love to you both.

Mc

SHADOWS...
An anthology of short stories

by

Oldham Writing Café Writers

OWC Publishing

First published in the UK 2010 by
OWC Publishing
P.O. Box 656
OLDHAM OL4 2SD

ISBN 978-0-9565410-0-0

Printed and bound in the UK by
Mqwikprint Design & Print
Milnsbridge, Huddersfield.

Financially supported by The Community Grant sponsored and
administered by Oldham Council and Voluntary Action Oldham.

FOREWORD

Everybody has memories and, no matter how misty they are, they leave their shadows on the present. Here are more than twenty very different short stories drawing on what the writers recall from their own pasts and what they have been told by a cross section of Oldhamers. Then vivid imaginations have been to work to create fiction worthy of the feisty spirit of local people.

Margaret Meehan
Secretary of Oldham Writing Café
2010

Without the funding provided from the Community Grant system supported and administered by Oldham Council and Voluntary Action Oldham, this project would not have been possible, so on behalf of all the Oldham Writing Café writers I would like to thank them for having faith in our "from Misty Memory to Feisty Fiction" project and providing the financial support for this book to have been published.

Carolyn Crossley
Chairman and Co-ordinator of Oldham Writing Café
2010

DEDICATION

Oldham Writing Café writers would like to dedicate this anthology to the memory of our late friend and fellow writer, Nigel Hague, with love.

CONTENTS

OLDHAM WRITING CAFÉ – THE AUTHORS

1.   Carolina de la Cruz, despite her pen name was born and bred in Oldham. Both a published and performance poet, (the Vixen of Verse) and fledgling playwright; she is currently adding to her portfolio of short stories. She would like 2010 to be the year she completes her first novel.

2.   Amanda Carr has been published in several short story anthologies, magazines and e-zines, and is a member of a large, international online writing community. Currently, she divides her time between family, writing and delivering creative writing workshops. She is a preferred author at Writing.Com under the pseudonym of Acme.

3.   Patricia Gray started writing at an early age for pure enjoyment. She is an avid reader which has contributed to her love of the written word. The Custodian and The Doorman are her first published works. She is currently working on a crime novel which will be completed later this year.

4.   Peggy Bottomley, whose mother's family has been long-established in Oldham, has been an avid teller of tales since childhood. This has been nourished by a love of reading, particularly fantasy, and of poetry, especially Keats and Browning.

5.   Lesley Truchet, was born in Leeds and has worked in administration roles in various parts of the UK and in France. Lesley always had a keen interest in literature, but only began writing seriously in 2008, just before joining the Oldham Writing Café. Since joining the café she has written a number of short stories and poems.

6. Maggie Nicholson has always enjoyed reading and story-telling. In this she was strongly influenced by her father who used his vivid imagination to turn quite every-day events into extraordinary adventures.

7. Carol Marie Higgins, was christened at Millgate Methodist Church, married at St. Margaret's Church, Hollins and until 15 years ago, lived and worked in the Hollins – Hollinwood areas. Carol's keen interest in creative writing enabled her to turn her memories into the fascinating glance into the past that constitutes her short story.

8. Marjory Travis is constantly aware of the debt she owes to her uncle who encouraged her love of reading and enlivened many a wet Sunday afternoon with his versions of the adventures of Tarzan.

9. Faye Burgess was born in Tasmania and has worked and travelled throughout Australia and as far as the remote highlands of Papua New Guinea. At that time she was the only white woman living and working in the village amidst a tribal war. Faye has many stories to write.

10. Nigel Hague, was a beloved father, grandfather and friend. He found an outlet for his creativity in writing but sadly left us before this story was published. This story is published in his memory to share his passion for writing and for his loved ones to be even more proud of him.

ACKNOWLEDGEMENTS

Thanks goes to all of the following people and organisations without whom this anthology would not have been produced and they are in "no particular order":

Amanda Carr, Pauline Clarke and Michael Davis the founding members of Oldham Writing Café,

The Community Grant System sponsored by both Oldham Council and Voluntary Action Oldham (VAO), our generous funders who liked the idea of our "From Misty Memory to Feisty Fiction project".

Patricia Gray for her skills and experience as mentor throughout the bid writing process.

Gemma Hall, our talented illustrator who designed the book cover.

Our editing team, of Amanda Carr, Lesley Truchet and led by the inimitable Margaret Meehan.

Mick Jacombs our printer, (mqwikprint@btconnect.com) who helped with the cover design, the layout of the book and was so enthusiastic about our project it was infectious!

Fr. David Hawthorn of the Parish of Saint Margaret's Church, Hollins, who welcomed our group both into his parish and church hall.

Andrew Barr of Saint Margaret's Church, Hollins who helped the less computer literate of the writers to grasp the basics of information technology.

The people who shared their memories with us, the misty and the not so misty!

Special thanks to "The Silver Ladies Group" from St. Margaret's church, who made research so much fun and plied us with coffee and cakes, and sang us songs from yesteryear.

Alan Davies, the Deputy Churchwarden of Saint Margaret's Church, Hollins.

Dorothy Nelson and Beverley Lees and their memories of Waterhead.

Thanks to the following websites for information on Castleshaw, the Roman Fort and the mysterious ghost that appeared in the sixties:
http://www.ukattraction.com/north-west-england/castle-shaw-reservoir-and-roman-fort.htm
http://www.oldham.gov.uk/castleshaw
http://www.mysteriousbritain.co.uk/england/greater-man-chester/hauntings/castleshaw-roman-camp-rigodunum.html

Russell Dawson, Norma Dunkerley, David Hazeltine, Margaret, George and Ellen Henry, John and Ellen Meehan, Molly Owen, Hilda Palmer and Alice Walvin.

Mum Burgess, Dad Burgess and John Conroy.

Sean Baggaley, who as the Local History Curator at Gallery Oldham inspired Amanda Carr to look more closely into Oldham's past in order to produce her four short stories.

And finally Punam Ramchurn, Literature Development Officer for Oldham Council who provided us with encouragement and a wonderful venue for our book launch.

AWAKENING

It was summer of 1969 and the weather was hot, Caitlin McKenna and her sister Brenda were wandering somewhat aimlessly down the ginnel that separated the back of the houses on Huddersfield Road and joined from Sharples Hall Street on one side to Equitable Street on the other. The ginnel was cobbled and had so far escaped a covering of tarmac that seemed to be spreading over every pavement in the district. The sisters lived in a house on Sharples Hall Street which just scraped into the Waterhead district whilst Equitable Street belonged to the new Littlemoor council estate. This mattered a lot to their mother who had ambitions to raise up her family from the imagined stigma of living on a council estate to the more privileged status of being a private home owner.

Both Mr. and Mrs. McKenna had worked hard to become home owners and were justifiably proud of their status. They wanted only the best for their daughters and had ambitions for them becoming teachers or white collar workers whilst the parents on the estate would just be glad to get their child in a job, any job. It wasn't that the McKennas were snobs, although others could be forgiven for thinking so. Mr. McKenna was originally from Northern Ireland. This fact alone enabled the estate dwellers to feel superior to him; the Irish were considered to be a race of tinkers. Even though Mrs. McKenna was quick to point out that her husband came from Northern Ireland and therefore was as British as they were, the estate people were too uneducated to know the difference. Although they all agreed what a fine man Mr. McKenna was and how he spoke with barely an accent at all.

The McKenna girls reached Equitable Street and crossed

over it and continued down the back to the grassed area that opened out behind the next block of terraced houses on Huddersfield Road.

"Look at that!" Brenda pointed excitedly at the tent that had been erected upon the grass facing the house on Huddersfield Road that belonged to the Beresford family.

"Wow, yes a tent!" Caitlin stated the obvious. "Do you think it belongs to the Beresfords?"

"Sure to, shall we go and see?"

Caitlin nodded by way of reply and they ran over to the tent to see if anyone was inside. Brenda encouraged her elder sister to open the flap and look inside. Caitlin hesitated a moment, at 14 years old there were a lot of things that frightened her, but of course it didn't do to show that to her sister, so she took a deep breath, dropped to her knees and lifted the flap up gingerly and peeped inside. A tall youth lay on his back in the tent filling it completely down one side. His eyes closed, Greg short for Gregory Beresford knew very well that he had company but chose to ignore the intrusion and see what would transpire.

Pestered by her sister, Caitlin withdrew her head and told her that Greg was there. Brenda wanted to know where the other Beresford boys were, and Caitlin suggested she go to the house and call for them. Brenda skipped off to the back gate of the Beresford's house and, finding it open, went in to knock on the back door and call for Brian and Harry, the two younger Beresford boys. Meanwhile Caitlin returned to her scrutiny of the prone figure of Greg Beresford. Greg was 17, tall with dark hair and handsome dark brown eyes. He had an athletic build from playing rugby and an easy, teasing manner when he spoke to girls, especially ones that fancied him and he knew that Caitlin McKenna fancied him. It amused him that Miss High and Mighty McKenna found him so irresistible.

"Are you going to stay there all day or come in?" he opened his eyes and asked at last.

He smiled as she blushed furiously and without further ado, crawled on her hands and knees into the tent to lie on the other side of it.

"What you got there?" he asked as she squirmed around bringing something out from under the cardigan that had been draped over her arm.

"It's a book." she stated, "It's called Wuthering Heights and it's by Emily Bronte, ever read it?"

"Who me? Nah, don't go in for girls' books."

"It's not a girls' book, it's a classic."

"Yeah, well I haven't read it, OK?"

"You can borrow it if you like, after I've read it of course."

"Nah, you're all right, I can live without reading it."

"Suit yourself!"

She lay on her tummy and opened the book and began to read it. Greg stretched and sat up. He could hear voices outside the tent and sure enough the flap opened and his brothers peered in to ask if he wanted to play cricket with them. He shook his head saying it was too hot. Caitlin asked if Brenda was with them only to be told she was playing at dolls with their younger sister, Linda in their house. Caitlin sighed and hoped that Greg wouldn't be persuaded to go and play cricket. The boys left them together whilst they set up the stumps and Greg leaned back on his elbows and surreptitiously watched the girl reading. He suspected that she was reading the same paragraph over and over as she had not turned a page in several minutes, either that or she wasn't reading at all.

He smirked a little thinking of the effect his nearness was having on the girl. She wasn't pretty but she wasn't ugly either and she had a budding pair of breasts, which stretched the fabric of her t-shirt provocatively, and long bare legs that he wanted to reach out and touch, just to feel her skin beneath his fingers. He imagined it would be soft and silky. He narrowed his eyes and watched as she finally turned the page. She ran her tongue over her lips and he imagined the feel of her tongue inside his mouth and felt the familiar stirrings of lust. He wasn't a virgin, far from it; since discovering sex he had embarked upon a steep learning curve and now he felt an irresistible attraction towards Caitlin McKenna.

A cricket ball hit the side of the tent just missing Greg's head by a whisper and he swore quietly, irritated at the interruption. Caitlin laughed and turned to face him and he knew that she had an inkling of what he had been thinking about. Now it was his turn to feel a little embarrassed.

"Oi! you lot be careful you nearly hit my bloody head!"

"Sorry Greg!" came the boys' reply in unison although they sounded anything but sorry and were both giggling uncontrollably.

"Bloody idiots!"

Caitlin smiled by way of reply and sat up and began rearranging her skirt pulling it down so she no longer revealed anything enticing.

Greg decided to make his move and leaned forward to kiss her, she saw it coming and closed her eyes and held her lips up to him, her whole body quivering with anticipation. His lips found hers and kissed her lightly on the lips and she instinctively drew her arms up to link them around his neck as she had seen women do on television, she not having had any personal experience to draw on. He pulled her closer and his arms imprisoned her against his body. She was struggling to get her breath and opened her mouth and he took the opportunity to probe her mouth with his tongue. His hands moved down her back and one of them found its way quickly to her breast and he felt her go limp in his arms, like a rag-doll. He began to massage her breast and she moaned beneath his kiss, opening her mouth to receive his probing tongue, and he knew that she wanted this, wanted him. Greg's fingers found her nipple and through the thin material of both her bra and t-shirt he squeezed until it hardened like a tight little rosebud and Greg felt filled with confidence at the effect he was having upon the girl.

Whack! Another cricket ball hit the tent, followed by more giggles and Greg broke away from Caitlin, his face flushed from his mounting sexual arousal. He held her at arms length, enjoying the almost mesmerised expression on her face confirming the impression that this was her first real kissing session. Whack! This time it was too much for Greg.

"That does it!" Greg was out of the tent and chasing his brothers who ran off one in each direction, leaving Caitlin to gather herself. When Greg returned she was lying on her tummy again supposedly reading her book, but he wasn't fooled. He stayed in the entrance crouching down with the tent flap in his hand.

"Come on we'll never get any peace with those two around and here comes your Brenda too."

Wordlessly Caitlin got up on her knees and crawled out of the tent as she had crawled in. As she passed him, he drew in his breath as he resisted the urge to reach out and touch the creamy white flesh of her exposed thighs. Instead he got to his feet and pulled Caitlin to hers.

"Why don't I take you to the pictures, tonight?"

"Pictures? Like a date, you mean?"

"Oh definitely like a date, on the back seat at the pictures and we can walk through the park on our way home."

"OK, but it will be dark in the park won't it, after the pictures?"

"Oh yes it most certainly will be." Greg laughed lasciviously.

"Maybe there will be moonlight, that will be romantic, won't it?"

"If you say so Caitie, if you say so." Romance was the last thing on Greg's fertile, sexually aroused mind.

Author's note

This story came about following a talk with my sister when she recently came to visit. Some of the incidents are factual and some pure figments of my imagination, the trick is to guess which is which!

Carolina de la Cruz

BLACKPOOL vs MANCHESTER

We came together in the summer, when the hornets were angry and the wasps were lazy, when the windows were wide open throughout the night, and the scent of honeysuckle and salt water were woven into the blanket of humidity against the skin.

Sat on the roof of the boarding house, we could choose between cider or elderberry wine. We chose both. Summer made our humanity take a back seat to the more pressing needs of animal survival. So, naturally, we began to bitch. About Barbara. About men. About the heat.

Selena had been making us laugh again. It had been her turn to cycle for rations and P.C. Scott had stopped her at Squires Gate. Having loaded up her basket with black market gammon joints for Uncle Bob, she had set off to return home on the family bicycle—with no brakes. We all knew how to stop the metal monster with our feet against the front tyre, but the loaded bike was so heavy, and Lena was so little, she'd just ridden straight over the cross roads. P.C. Scott had given her a five-shilling fine but Uncle Bob hadn't clipped her. After all, the helpful policeman had insisted in steering her home with a bike full of illegal pork products. They thanked him for his help and hung the ham in the attic.

As the sun set over South Shore Pier our little group raised its glasses and watched the resident RAF boys file out into Blackpool to do battle with the American lads on the dance floor of the Tower Ballroom. The prize? The easy favours of a Manchester girl out for the night and a pair of silk stockings.

"Right then, Cissy." Mary turned to me and popped half a cigarette between my lips. "Me first."

This said, she kicked off her shoes, pulled her skirt up and tucked it into her knickers. Selena opened the tin of gravy browning and began rubbing it smoothly over Mary's legs to create a pair of stockings, and I dipped a sliver of charcoal in to my cider ready to run a seam down her legs. We three always wore the best silk stockings in town, until it rained. The trick was to wear a dark skirt on the dance floor.

Even though the pink glow of evening had darkened to violet, the heat had not diminished. The air hung heavy and hit back as we pushed our way next to the dance floor. Selena's light brown curls bobbed away through the throng of tables for a few minutes and then returned triumphant. In the crook of her arm she had acquired three, very nearly full, pop bottles from a deserted table. As we toasted each other, she yelped, eyes filled with panic, by the authoritative hand placed on her shoulder.

"Wouldn't you ladies prefer your own drinks?" came an amused voice.

"Oh, Tony Gommer!" Selena chided him, slapping his hand away in mock disgust. "You shouldn't go creeping up on folk; people will think you have gone daft."

"I have!" He laughed at her. "Want to dance?"

She grinned, pressed her pop bottle into Mary's hand and turned into his arms. The dance floor swallowed them.

I slurped my pop, and watched the bumping, jumping, energy of the dancers with Mary. Not for long, though. Mary had hair like Veronica Lake and sure enough an adoring circle of manly laughter began to gather around her. I was just about to go and find another lemonade when

I found my way blocked by Barbara Jones. Red hair, green eyes and Betty Grable legs all the way up to here. No-one liked her. We hated her. She seemed to take a perverse delight in tormenting Mary - her only real competitor.

"Let me guess..." She grinned, like a cat playing with it's dinner. "This week you're from—Rochdale? You need some rich Yankee to take you to the station. He'll give you some smokes and chocolate, and you'll give him a quick kiss goodbye. This I gotta see, Cissy."

"Actually, we're from Salford," I retorted, then realised I'd given the game away. How did she do that? Her lips twitched in pleasure, she arched her eyebrow and broke in to Mary's circle.

"Mary! What a surprise." She hugged her, "Oh, you better hurry, dear - the last train to Manchester will be here in twenty minutes."

A look of bewildered confusion crossed Mary's face before I crashed in on them. "Yes, Barbara's right," I gently pulled her hand, "we better go."

A bright, pine scented chin jutted in on me, "Don't you worry now, miss." He smiled, ushering our group toward the door. "My boys'll escort you to the station. You won't miss your train; we'll make sure of that."

***

Our feet hurt. Mary leaned on me while she knocked the stones from her shoes on an old styal.

"I hate Barbara," she muttered, and we set off again, back

toward Blackpool from the Kirkham station, five miles away.

"Me too," I agreed through barely parted, sugared lips, "but this American candy makes up for it."

She smiled and ruffled my hair, laughing.

"Same again next weekend, Cissy. Same again."

Author's Note

My grandmother is 93 years old. She was born a White-Rose in Barnsley and worked for the family in a Blackpool boarding house during the war where she met her husband. She would tell tales of doing battle on the dance floor with the Manchester girls who came to party hard. She was most amused to end up spending a huge chunk of her life as one of them in Red-Rose country.

Amanda Carr

CANAL KNOWLEDGE

I stood firmly to attention. My ribcage jutted out beyond my chin, my stomach compressed against my backbone, and my lungs stung to capacity. I felt ten feet tall and full of pride as I stood shoulder to shoulder with my equally proud peers and watched the launch of the HMS Pirate's Blood.

It was probably the finest craft ever to set sail on the Huddersfield Narrow Canal, and it had taken us since Easter to engineer. My eyes were still drawn to the beautiful, lobster-blue nylon washing line that cost a hiding and a ripped pair of shorts to procure.

The line bound the mast to the pallet-board decking and stretched all the way up the broom handle to Grandpa Jack's bloodstained handkerchief. He once told us it was enemy blood that he had dipped his hanky in during the war, but Nan had rolled her eyes and said, "Sure... If the enemy was the fool in the mirror with a cut-throat razor."

My two brothers nodded solemnly in my direction to indicate that I should prepare to test the sea worthiness of the vessel. Oar in hand, I tentatively tested the deck with my tiptoe, before Christian laughed and propelled me forward with a shove. I regained my pride and my footing nearly instantly as the raft turned gently and I found myself swaying on top of the oily black water.

"It floats!" Mathias exclaimed, jubilantly.

"Of course it does," Christian dead-panned. He threw a little bundle of provisions at me and took a running jump from the bank onto the raft. Mathias grabbed the mooring rope and jumped on too, causing The Pirate's Blood to dip alarmingly to port until Captain Christian righted us.

Mathias had thoughtfully constructed a little wheel from an old go-cart at the bow to allow me to pretend to steer us. It also kept me away from the water, because he knew I couldn't swim. It meant that he and Christian could get on with the more important jobs, like pushing us away from the banks and steering us safely over reed beds as we looked for opportunities to plunder.

I sat cross legged by my steering post and battered a wasp away from the jam sandwich given to me. I was having a bite to push down every mouthful of rum that was passed my way. It was awful and I could see my brothers wincing at the passage of the spicy liquor down their throats, but we were obliged to do it if we didn't want to get thrown out of the Pirate's Navy. That said, I wasn't sure that real pirates drank 'Bay Rum Hair Tonic' from Grandpa Jack's medicine cabinet.

As we negotiated the lock at Slaithwaite I was given hooks to bait while Christian and Mathias argued over whether or not fish existed in the canal. By the time we neared Marsden it was decided that normal fish didn't populate the depths. This was the domain of the terrifying Giant Yorkshire Squid and we should be thankful to not have had a bite for the last hour.

Darkness was flooding inky stains across the landscape and I was tired. Mathias lifted my sleepy body from the raft and onto the bank of the retiring village of Diggle. Christian led us around the enemy streets.

"Are we nearly home?" I enquired, nervously.

"No whining, now," Christian reminded me. "We could be in Lancashire and you haven't got your passport."

I pressed my lips together firmly and nodded, letting him navigate us past stone houses and gritty mill walls until, finally, we saw the blue light in the distance and all sighed with relief.

The round-faced policeman at the desk looked up as we came in and then smiled upon recognising our dirty, urchin faces.

"Put some cocoa on, Sam." he instructed the back office. "We've been invaded by the Yorkshire Vikings again."

"Pirates, this time," I corrected him, "and we need your treasure and your ginger biscuits."

Author's note

One of my favourite days out with the writers from Oldham Writing Cafe was a summer day trip on the canal. Our canal boat was full of laughter, memories, good food, and stories. The day seemed to fly by, as a memorable, if sedate, adventure, even if we did steer into the bank on a number of occasions. The canals were the life-blood of the Industrial North and are still a wonderful part of Oldham and the surrounding area's historical legacy, as well as great recreational fun.

Amanda Carr

"Oh God," wailed Tantillus the smallest angel.

A red aura swirled towards him.

"Stop that, stop that now. We never mention Him; he senses your concern and it is worrisome for Him, do you understand?" questioned Mortum, her powerful thought sounds vibrating with authority. "As Custodian of the Death Register, it is my duty to deal with this matter."

"Yes, yes, sorry, sorry. It is just that I feel pain when earthlings make living wills that state, 'should I not be able to be resuscitated without having full mental and physical capabilities, I claim my right to instruct that any machines keeping me alive be turned off,'" he intoned in what he thought was the voice of a human earthling and. in fact, were inaudible waves floating on sound vibrations to Mortum.

Mortum's form shuddered.

"I know. Utter chaos follows these instructions, but how can humans know that to pre-empt their death time jeopardises their soul and brings pain and torment to others." Mortum floated in the direction of the earth viewer where moving pictures showed a young woman listening intently to a young man sitting across from her. Mortum adjusted the sound waves to counteract the universal vibrations. The sound waves of the young man's voice floated across to Tantillius and Mortum.

"Let me make this clear," said the young solicitor kindly. "A traditional will speaks from death, for the dead. A living will is different." He pointed at the papers lying on the desk between them. "The Testator, that's the person who has made the will, is still alive and seeks to anticipate the circumstances leading up to death or even empowering death, but in either case the will, can be challenged."

Tantillus and Mortum quivered pinkly.
"And that's all he thinks happens?"
Mortum's thoughts vibrated, as a wave undulated down her form.
"Heaven wrap your bonds around us," sighed Tantillus.
But Mortum was lost on another thought plane and did not react to this blasphemy.

"We have to take action Tantillus."
Mortum elongated her form decisively.
Tantillus froze, "Action! We cannot do that. He will kill us."
Tantillus became a mass of quivering spikes and Mortum's form turned red, a sign of irritation and anger.
"We are already dead," Mortum's form peaked in agitation at the edges, "He can only smite us."
"I do not like to be smitten, I wi…."
"That is enough Tantillus." Mortum turned a deeper shade of red, her thoughts flowing onto passing sound waves. "This woman's name is not written in the Death Register of pre-emptors," pulsed Mortum softly. "Therefore, if she follows through with her decision to decide the time of her death she will take the place allocated to another human. This human will have to stay on earth longer. They could be in pain, or confined in torment, praying for release. "Defying the Death Register of pre–emptors will trigger events which will have an adverse effect not only on this woman, but on other humans both physically and emotionally close to her. The Orbis of Aqua will also begin to waver and the ripple effect will be devastating. We will act together, Tantillus, to address this imbalance and so prevent tears, anguish and self hatred."
Mortums's aura swirled pale pink as the red thoughts began

27

to evaporate on the calm waves of her impeccable logic.

The thoughts of Tantillus bobbed up and down between the waves, as he struggled to join together the complex elements of Mortum's reasoning. "In all the millennia we have been together you have always followed the dictate of the Orbis of Aqua, by staying aloof, and apart from conflict. So why now?" The swirling energy of Tantillus became calm and still, as he waited patiently for an answer.

Mortum circled Tantillius her white energy folding Tantillius within the swirls.
"This is true, small one. I have been a loyal servant to Him, never questioning or allowing time, circumstances or injustice to trouble my unfathomable consciousness; but something has happened; I have begun to feel again." Tantillus would have gasped had he had that capability, instead the aura around him spiked at the edges. "Feel," he vibrated as the spikes elongated and retracted in silent rhythm. "Then your time is coming." "Yes Tantillius, my cosmic time is coming allowing me one chance to be Him and feel again human emotions."

Mortum drifted over to the earth viewer, the couple were frozen in the same position, as when she had last viewed them. She flashed an arrow of white light into the viewer causing the papers which lay on the desk like a silent observer to flutter slightly, as though to signal that it was time to move the conversation on.

"I didn't realise something I had thought about in advance and thought was lawful because it was through a solicitor, could be challenged." The girl was showing signs of agitation. "I thought I was doing the right thing for my

28

immediate family and anyone else likely to come into my life in the future."

The young man shook his head sympathetically. "People don't realise there are limitations to living wills. For example you can't ask for your life to be ended or force doctors to act against their professional judgement." "What if I nominated someone else to decide about treatment on my behalf?" the girl asked. The solicitor sighed. "No, you can't do that either. The concept of a living will, or making advance decisions as they are sometime called, seems like a good idea, but there are many difficulties."

There was silence in the room as the girl absorbed what had been said to her. She closed her eyes; jumping when the young man's voice broke into her thoughts. "Why do you want to make advance decisions about dying? What's driving you to plan the end of your life at thirty two?" The girl shrank back into her seat as though moving away from a physical presence emanating from the question.

"My mum died last year suffering from multiple sclerosis and my sister has the disease," she whispered. "And I see the way my dad is being worked into the ground caring for her day in and day out. I help, of course I do, but I'm a young woman with a career to follow and a life to unfold yet. A life I must try to live to the full before I get the disease, and when I get it, if life has been good to me and I have met the love of my life, I don't want to see him or any children we may have burdened with looking after me."

The young man leaned forward to catch the last words which were hoarsely forced out, as the girl struggled with her emotions. He held out his hands in silent sympathy and the girl placed hers into them.

As she watched the young couple, the deep turquoise of understanding began to swirl around Mortum.

 "The Orbis of Aqua is beginning to open and the Alchemist awakens. I must act soon to prevent oceans of tears and fathomless depths of guilt flowing and forming around this man and women."

Tantillius still vibrating from the revelation of Mortum's cosmic future began to energy melt into the palest of turquoise radiating from Mortum as the beginnings of understanding encompassed his psyche.

"I don't yet fully understand your meaning Mortum. Has not the woman's destiny been foretold and therefore something you cannot affect?"

"You are right and wrong," flowed Mortum. "Although our powers are great we cannot use them against destiny's dictate which is irrevocable; what is foretold will take place. But this woman's name is not written in the Death Register of the pre-emptors, her destiny is not to choose the time of her death.

Consequently I am not going against destiny's dictate. The complication is the Alchemist. To satisfy his desire to inject grief and suffering into the lives of humans he will try to link into my business as Custodian of the Death Register.

But I have a way to change the fate he has planned."

"There will be a death." Vibed Tantillius.

Mortum did not respond her concentration was on pulling the earth viewer towards her on waves of radiance power.

"Look at the time lapse Tantillius, earth's rotation has moved on two years.

See the changes time has wreaked."

 On the earth viewer, the man and women were locked in a passionate embrace.

Their hands stroking each others limbs leaving no doubt

as to the familiarity each felt for the other's body.

The woman broke free pushing the man's arms away. "No, no, you always win me round with melting embraces and passion.

Over the years it has always been the same; I don't know how you bear the guilt of your deceit." She cried contemptuously. "Well I do," the woman answered herself.

"You drown yourself in passion and take me with you, but it is going to stop now." She uttered the time honoured words of adulterers the Universe over.

"You can either leave your wife and child to be with me, or we part forever."

Mortum shivered and spiralled flame red. "The Alchemist has seized the moment to use his corrosive chemistry. I ought to have thrown a shield around this couple whilst I stilled the Orbis of Aqua; now a third human and a very small child are caught in the Orbis." The form of Tantillius swirled pinkly.

"But Mortum, surely this means the death register must be filled."

"Most definitely small one, but first I need to restore life from the pain and sorrow his repulsive chemistry has caused."

The earth viewer clouded then cleared. A woman was weeping. The flowing tears followed the curve of her cheeks to wet her lips which were pressed against the soft hair of the sleeping child on her knee. The man stood in the doorway watching, pain etched into the lines on his face as looked at the child he loved and adored asleep in his mothers arms. The child he was about to stop living with day to day; the child who would grow and learn about life with minimal input from its father. "Don't go", said the woman. "Stay with us, have your affair and keep it discreet; I can live with that, only please don't leave us." She choked as tears caught in her throat. "I promise I will never ask where you are going or where you have been, I promise." she sobbed.

The man was crying "I have to go, I can't go on like this, you can't go on like this, you deserve better than me, you need someone to make you happy and that's not me." He finished lamely.

"Behold the gravity of deception, Tantillius." Mortum flowed and swayed in front of the earth viewer. "The Alchemist's work is rooted in the practice of achieving wisdom with intellectual links to many communities, Kabbalism, spiritualism, cryptology and others, amongst them white and black witchcraft. It is the black arts he is using now to manipulate time and events, so we must move through time Tantillius and close the Aqua, before eternal damage is done," vibed Mortum as they floated to the earth viewer.

The pictures on the viewer were surreal. It was night; flashing lights shed by emergency vehicles shone on the wet road, giving a dream like quality to the scene. A car lay upside down, the roof crushed and twisted. As Mortum and Tantillius watched a women was lifted gently from the twisted wreckage by paramedics. It was the living will woman. She was quickly fitted with life support equipment. A bleeping monitor showed the vibrant strength of her heartbeats.

The woman's face was peaceful. All the pain and concern was etched on the face of the man attending her.
"I don't like the look of this at all." He turned to his companion. "I think she may have concussion and if the damage to the car roof is anything to go by it's critical. Come on, Joe," he shouted to the driver, "let's get her out of here and into casualty."

The earth viewer clouded over.

"It begins," flowed Mortum, as she moved to the viewer. "Let us watch Tantillius and see the perfidious nature of man struggle to bring about redemption for himself, peace for one woman and joy for the other."

The man was sitting at the bedside of his wife who was lying still. Wires and machines pulsed life into her and the bleep of the monitoring machines counted the passing of time. Mercifully their small son had been taken to play in the crèche and was spared this harrowing sight. A young man entered. The badge on his shirt showed him to be a doctor. He stood quietly by the seated man and spoke softly, " Your wife has suffered years with this heart condition, but over the last few months her condition has deteriorated. Unless we find a new heart within the next forty eight hours her chances of survival are very slim." The seated man closed his eyes. "I don't understand why this is happening?"

he moaned, looking up at the doctor. "The medication suited her making her condition stable, allowing her to pursue a full and active life."

The doctor shook his head. "I don't understand it either. You can imagine I have seen some things in my time, people pulling back from the brink of death, healthy people lapsing into comas, but this," he waved his hand in the manner of a benediction over the still form of the women. "This is inexplicable. It is as if her heart has suddenly started shrinking, which is impossible, quite impossible." He shook his head as if clearing his mind of such nonsense.

The earth viewer picture clouded and in their space the watching Tantillius and Mortum floated peacefully in the palest of blue light.

"Ah now I understand and see your way Mortum. It is

you who are the wife's fluttering heart, staying the hand of the Alchemist. When the Alchemist wanted death at the car accident, you are the heart that beats defiantly in the living will women. You are holding time still", quivered Tantillius. "Who do we wait for Mortum?"
"We wait Tantillus for the man to redeem himself with an act so loving both women and the boy will know love, peace and joy."
Mortum's thoughts swayed within the peaceful blue light as she readied herself to move over time zones.

Mortum stretched effortlessly through the earth viewer and across the time barrier; to meld into the one they called the doctor. Looking through his eyes, Mortum gazed at the anguished face of the seated man as she forced her thought waves into his weaker human brain. "You have a hard choice to make." The lips of the doctor remained still, but the man could hear the words quite clearly. "Your mistress lies along the corridor in a critical coma. Her brain is quite dead, but her heart beats strongly with life. Many years ago you advised her against making a living will. Your reasoning was sound and based around the fact that multiple sclerosis is not genetic and therefore she was unlikely to contract it. She however was not convinced and sought counsel with another solicitor. He in turn supported your advice, and the outcome was she made a traditional will, which included a clause covering organ donation should she meet with any unforeseen accident."

The man on the chair listened calmly to the thought waves of Mortum, shock and agitation only becoming visible at Mortum's next words.
"As you know, your mistress has recently been experiencing body malfunctions which, without consulting a doctor, she took to be the start of multiple sclerosis. Without going into

34

great detail her accident was self induced, causing her to become a pre-emptor, someone who tries to die before her time. This means she has forfeited special peace in the spaces."

"No," said the man jumping up from his chair. "No, she would never do that after all the heartache we caused others so we could be together, she would never leave me, never."

His hands covering his face, the man cried softly. Mortum's thought waves pushed out to him relentlessly.

"She has no next of kin and in the will she has named you as executor. Soon you will have to take on that role. The doctors will look to you to support any decision they may take regarding the condition of your mistress. Think hard human. Your wife needs the heart of your mistress to bring her back from the brink of death. You owe your wife the right to fulfil her role as mother to your son and wife to you. That's if she will have you." Mortums's voice pulsed softly.

"Try to understand, there are spaces beyond this world, spaces to which we must all return in the end, and you need to ensure your own space is with the redeemers. Delegation to a space is correlated to your actions on this earth. The Orbis of Aqua or as you know it, the Circle of Life, demands this segmentation, to single out right and wrong. Your mistress is in jeopardy; the wrong decision now, will send her into the dark space of the pre- emptors. Think hard, human."

Mortum passed back through the viewer to join Tantillius. "Do you think you have succeeded in making the man understand, Mortum?"

"Who can say when you are dealing with beings so under-developed?" she mused as she floated peacefully in the palest of blue calm.

"Let us hope the man will move fast as I cannot go back and correct any mistakes that are made."

"Look, look at the Death Register." Vibed Tantillius excitedly as he turned a deep shade of pink. "The woman's name has just appeared there; the woman who wanted a living will."

His thought waves came to an abrupt end as they encountered a mass of angry red power, so strong and wide it filled the space around both Mortum and himself.

"You have interfered in my plans Mortum," spiked the Alchemist. "You will pay dearly for this."
Mortum used all her pure white power to expand higher and wider than the Alchemist forcing the red violence to bunch tighter for protection against Mortum's authority
"And how shall I pay?" she spiked ceaselessly. "Your powers are less than mine and He will not allow discord of this magnitude."

"You will be denied cosmic creation for crossing the time line," vibed the Alchemist, his psychic presence growing in confidence and pushing against the white power of Mortum. "There is no precedent for what you did; you have broken every barrier with your interference in the life of humans."

"And you," said Mortum, pushing ferociously against the encroaching red essence.

"You think you are going to prevent my right of passage to becoming a cosmic entity? You, who have broken the sacrosanct rule of the Universe, the rule imposed by Him for all entities to live by, 'Thou must not kill'."

Mortum's energy patterns swirled encircling the Alchemist, causing his aura to spin erratically.

"Only He can stop the cosmic process and He will never break the eternal rule of Orbis. You forget that feeling emotion for humans is part of the cosmic journey.

You have failed Alchemist," vibed Mortum, her pure whiteness intensifying, overpowering the burning red of the Alchemist's entity as she increased her speed around the edges of his aura. He will not countenance your planting the desire for death through self harming in a human mind. Be gone you abomination, you betrayer of eternal rest."

The Alchemist's aura shuddered once before the momentum of Mortum's spinning energy caused him to explode and soar like an earthly sky rocket into the blackness of space. Mortum and Tantillius glided as one over to the earth viewer.

The man was looking down on the face of the woman he had met twelve years ago and taken as his mistress. Right from the beginning he had been honest with her making it clear he would never leave his wife and son. But as love had overtaken desire, engulfing them, enfolding them into each others hearts, he had taken the tortured decision to leave his marriage. How young she looks he thought, stroking her soft hair, not in the least ready for death and yet the doctor said the police were satisfied by the evidence at the scene of the accident. The tyre marks on the road, the angle of the car where it had hit the gable end of the house they said, all pointed to her deliberately aiming her car at the wall. Why? Why? His eyes squeezed shut in pain and he dropped his chin onto his chest. She had been happy, or so he thought, the spectre of Multiple Sclerosis eradicated as she had learned more about the disease and realised it was not genetic.

Her initial guilt that a child had been left fatherless because of her need had faded as time passed by. Although she had once said that not many people commit adultery with impunity. Maybe she thought the recent aches and pains were Multiple Sclerosis, risen from the dead as punishment for her long ago sin. The man lifted his head. The doctor, who had been standing quietly in the shadows, stepped forward and nodded to him that it was time. Time for one last kiss on warm lips, one last touch at the corner of the mouth that could light up a room, as it curved into a heart stopping smile. "Goodbye," he touched the soft cheek. "Safe journey, my darling love." He ran his fingers across her forehead. "I will miss you until the last breath goes from my body," was his whispered prayer, as he gently touched his lips to hers. The machine which gave her body life went silent. A soft sigh escaped her mouth, her chest went still.

"She's gone", said the doctor softly.

The man rested his head against hers and wept.

The operation theatre hummed with the sound of machines taking on the role of the human heart. The silent team of doctors worked in concentration as the new heart was placed gently into the waiting cavity. Two hours later the chief surgeon raised her sweat drenched face. "We have a successful match, turn off the machine and let the new heart take over."

Mortum and Tantillius drifted within pale blue radiance as they watched the drama of human life via the earth viewer. Suddenly Mortum rose in an elongated line radiating white around her edges. "I can feel His presence," she vibed softly. "Go Tantillius this is no place for you just now."

"Peace is yours, Mortum, for eternity," exhaled Tantillius, as his form became smaller vaporising into atmospheric space. The palest blue light filled the space around Mortum, growing bigger and wider as the space around her expanded, leaving her looking small and insignificant.

"Oh Mortum. You chose a strange human story to trigger the feeling process again, a story as old as time itself and wrought with passion. A story to rip the emotions to shreds. You did well; you salvaged three lives and saved an innocent soul from the dark space. For although this woman did wrong and broke my commandment, 'thou shall not commit adultery', she did work tirelessly nursing children during the war in the Middle East, and for those acts of courage and selflessness she deserved to go into the space of the redeemers. "As for the Alchemist, there is no redemption for him." The pale blue essence throbbed and expanded. "Urging death desire and placing a soul in danger of becoming a pre-emptor will not do. Orbis has sealed the fate of the Alchemist. There is no room for the black arts here in our eternal space. He will go back to earth to be reborn again and face the trials and tribulations of human life." The aura of the Presence engulfed Mortum drawing her to the centre of his entity.

"And what of my cosmic time?" queried Mortum, her white form trembling within the soothing embrace of the Presence.

"Is upon you my good servant; it is time for you to go." The pale blue light turned darker at the edges. "Peace is yours Mortum for eternity."

The entity that was Mortum quivered and pulsed. Her pure white energy became for a nano second a blinding white light illuminating the pale blue heavens, before becoming one with the infinity of space.

  Watching from far away, Tantillius oscillated around the bright stars which formed part of the outer galaxy on the edge of infinity. A fierce pale blue light focused on his essence guiding him back to the earth viewer. The Presence signed for him to look into its depths.

"Behold the earth Tantillius," vibed the Presence. The man was walking by the sea, a young boy holding tightly to his hand. The boy looked up at the man's face and gave him a wide grin. The man looked down and smiled. "Such a wonderfully soul stopping action the smile," flowed the Presence softly, "but within its depths there is infinite power. There is the power to change the mood of the giver, and also the mood of the receiver. A miracle was wrought at the time of this evolutionary change in facial expression; a wondrous communication advancement for humans." The Presence folded Tantillus in calm waves as the smallest angel pulsed softly at the human scene before him. He watched as the man's wife waved at her family from the sand dunes, a smile reaching her eyes and lighting up her face. By her side a toddler dug chubby fingers into the wet sand.

With sparks of blue peace lights emanating from his energy, the Presence began to soar towards the infinity of space. "Mortum will be at peace with her actions in this matter," he pulsed. "Her logic and studied thought have smoothed her way into cosmic time."
The blue lights pulsed benignly.
"But what fate will befall the Alchemist?" vibed Tantillius, trying his hardest to keep up with the lightening speed of the Presence.
In answer, a long vapour of pure white light emanated from the Presence. Rising high and wide it moved at speed across space, the light momentarily penetrating the darkest outer regions beyond the knowledge of mankind, moving at light speed before disappearing into the blackness.

Tantillius was buffeted sideways and upwards, before floating downwards to safety, into the sound waves of wisdom left by His Presence. An echoing answer to his question lingered within the waves.

"Vengeance is mine."

Author's Note

The inspiration for this story came from a conversation I overheard in The Three Crowns public house on Huddersfield Road. Two women at the next table were discussing making a will. After several minutes during which they discussed what sort of message they would leave for loved ones, not so loved ones and hated ones. They started to discuss what if. What if an accident left one in a coma? The following discussion left both in no doubt, they agreed a living will was a "great idea". However their "what if," planted the germ of an idea in my mind from which Mortum and Tantillius were born. So ladies, should you recognise your conversation I would like to take this opportunity to say thank you and swear I will never reveal the names of the "hated ones" to be named in your wills.

Patricia Gray

DAWNING

Once upon a time, just before dawn on a cold October day, a woman walked her dog towards the ruined valley, the sole remnant of the faery land of her childhood. Her mood was as grey as the light for her children now stepped independently into the world, her workplace had no use for her, her love had gone, and her spirit ached from the wound.

She took the uneven rubble path, past the disembowelled dustbins spilling their sordid contents, past the carcases of supermarket trolleys, past the skeletons of forgotten buildings, to the turn in the path that showed her the extent of the council-funded massacre of her dream world. She stepped carefully to avoid the blocks of concrete half hidden by the rank grass, like fractured tombstones, ready to trip the unwary. The pewter coloured puddles in the ruts scowled at the lowering sky.

Suddenly the sun rose over her right shoulder, tinting the edges of the clouds with rose. The scrubby bushes and fledgling trees blazed in shades of flame, russet and gold; the brown water of the myriad tiny streamlets danced and chattered merrily. The plain stretched before her. The profile of the distant hills was shrouded in rags of mist. The air was clear. Her heightened senses picked up the phantom whir of the long gone windmill and the scent of wood smoke from the vanished farm. The ripples on the pond dazzled silver.

A movement caught her eye. Her love strolled towards her through the tussocks of the abandoned meadow with all the insouciance of youth. He was clad colourfully in a loose shirt and trousers, garments he would formerly have dismissed as fancy dress, but his eyes smiled into hers as they always had and his face was glorious.

"Greetings, my love, my heart, my wife."

She heard him with the ears of her soul and she ached to run to him, to fling herself into his arms, but his gesture halted her.

"I know you miss me, long for me and I feel your grief. For me it is different. I am no longer in time as you are. You cannot touch me. You must wait, for you have a task that you, and you alone, can do. Soon you will know it. Then, when you have finished, when you too are ready to escape from time, I will come for you, my own."

Just behind him came a fallow deer with her two fawns browsing the grass and then bounding effortlessly across the stream. Soundlessly a skein of geese rose from the pond and arrowed towards the north. They both turned to look.

When she brought her gaze back she was alone. She choked back a sob. Three magpies darted to the trees followed swiftly by another and above, in the chilly air, a kestrel hung. A few late flowers glowed on the gorse; in the grass tiny blossoms of daisy, clover and vetch braved the breeze; on the marshy bank clumps of sedge flaunted violet plumes; cushions of vivid moss flourished and flowered in damp crevices; sun-bleached grass stems danced with eccentric grace, and somewhere in a thicket a robin sang his defiance to the world.

She breathed deeply the sharp green smell of morning grass. She looked around and saw the spots of beauty pushing through the dross. Her heart filled with joy.

Author's note

Walking my dog down into Beal Valley and Broadbent Moss I was struck by the contrast between the mess left by the landfill preparation for the planned golf course and the richness of the wildlife, both plant and animal, that continues to flourish.
The version of the magpie rhyme I refer to;-
One for sorrow, two for mirth,
Three for a wedding, four for a birth.
Or in this case rebirth for a person rendered impotent by grief.

Peggy Bottomley

DILEMMA

She sat perfectly still, only her chest gently rising and falling belying the fact that she was a living, breathing human being. Or was she? She was no longer certain of what she was any more. What sort of human being just sat there immobile after what she had seen? She heard the low moaning coming from the nearby trees and still she remained sitting on the bench hoping it would stop, hoping it would go away.

He lay unmoving on the cold wet ground. He was a young man, about 24 years old. He was quite tall, of slim build, and he was mixed race and had short cropped dark hair, dark brown eyes and rather full, sensuous lips. He felt cold, that bone chilling cold when you feel like your life is draining out of your body drop by drop. The autumn leaves around him gave off a dank, foetid odour. He found himself shivering uncontrollably. He tried to make his mouth form the word, 'help' but found he was unable to do even that. Instead he moaned as a wave of pain hit him. The pain was excruciating. Why wouldn't the watching woman come and help him? He was sure someone was nearby, he had seen a woman sitting on the bench only about 30 or so yards away when he had arrived at the cemetery earlier on. How long ago was that now he wondered and tried to see the watch on his wrist. It took him all his strength to raise his wrist a couple of inches until he was able to see the paler skin of where his watch usually sat. The bastards had even taken his watch!

The woman sighed, surely she should go over and see if the young man was all right? She could see the shape of him lying beneath the edge of the copse of trees and bushes, he was as still as she was but, there, she could hear it again, that low moaning almost snatched away now by the sound of the wind which was getting up. She felt cold and pulled her scarf more tightly around her neck, trying to stop her body heat from escaping. It really wasn't the sort of weather for sitting in the cemetery, it was far too cold and damp. It was something she had done all summer long and into autumn, she found it soothing just to sit on the same bench every time, gazing into the middle distance. She allowed memories to flit in and out of her mind like a disjointed film reel. She was a tall, slender woman with brown hair that she kept dyed to keep the grey in it covered. She was in her early fifties and suffered from oesteo-arthritis in most of her joints making people think she was older because she was reduced to using a walking stick. She believed that pain aged people. This was the main reason she wore make up and carried a jazzy, brightly patterned walking stick to keep age at bay but she was not sure if she was successful or not. She brought her attention back to the prone figure, what should she do?

The young man lay not moving, his hand fallen back into the pile of leaves he was lying amongst. He was finding it more and more difficult to breath and he could hear his heart beating so fast that he was afraid it was going to burst out of his chest. He was desperately trying to remember what had happened to him, why he was in such pain, but he could feel his hold on consciousness slipping away. It was tempting to give into it and allow himself to fall into the beckoning black abyss.

Well, if she wasn't going to help him, she ought to get going, she thought. She was getting so cold sitting here and what if someone else came along and saw her? What would they think? What would they say? Not that many people did walk through the cemetery but there were workmen, groups of college students using it as a short cut, the occasional pair of lovers, whatever. She should get going. She mentally shook off her apathy and got slowly and painfully to her feet. She needed the assistance of her walking stick and the back of the bench to lever herself upright. The arthritis in her joints creaked out their protest as she set her body in motion after sitting for so long. She took two or three experimental steps leaning on her walking stick.

The young man started back into consciousness; from the corner of his eye he detected movement from the bench. Thank goodness she was coming to help him. He tried again to make his mouth form words and this time he managed a strangled sound that sounded like,' help me, help me!' Surely she would come over now and help him? He tried to raise his head to see if he could see her better and saw instead the hilt of a knife sticking out of his chest. There was blood oozing out from the entry wound and it had soaked into his clothing in a large dark wet stain. He let out a long low animal like screech as realisation set in. He had been stabbed, he was bleeding and maybe, just maybe, he was dying. Panic began to rise in his chest at the thought of impending death. Tears started to flow down his cheeks warm and salty, he didn't want to die, not here, not now.

The woman had started walking away from the bench when despite the growing noise of the wind she heard his sounds of fear and distress. She stopped, waiting to see if she could identify the next sound, it was not long in coming. Another agonised moan, containing the desperate words, help me, help me! Then she heard the young man's weeping, she sighed. She had witnessed an attack, a vicious attack, the young man outnumbered three to one. He hadn't stood a chance really. She had seen the glint of metal as the knife had been produced and despite the distance she had seen it being plunged into his chest. She had taken a sharp intake of breath, yet she had remained where she was, a silent and unwilling witness to a crime. She couldn't just leave him could she? It would be inhuman wouldn't it? She believed that she had come to know his type and whatever he had done to incite the others to such violence; she felt that he had deserved it. How could he be a victim? And yet, she hesitated she couldn't just walk away, could she?

His weeping struck a chord, how many times had she wept in the last year? Times too many to count; she hadn't realised that a person could cry that many tears, on and on, like a raging river of sadness and grief that swept away everything in its path, including, so it would seem, any compassion that may have lurked in the back of her mind. She had been compassionate once, but now? No there was no room now for compassion only the burning need for revenge. She wanted an eye for an eye, a tooth for a tooth or whatever else it said in the bible, that's what she wanted now, revenge to assuage her pain, her grief, her anger.

Still she hesitated, she couldn't just leave could she? Could she?

Author's Note

This story evolved from a discussion with my mother; we asked each other to what lengths grief could drive a person. It is based on personal grief, which is the memory part, but the rest is pure conjecture.

Carolina de la Cruz

"By heck, its cold tonight; give us a fag to warm me hands on, Jonesy," said Billy stamping his feet as he hunched his shoulders deeper into his overcoat. "It's that quiet out on that club door tonight I need something to do." Billy sighed as he watched the first punters of the night roll up. "I'm that bored I'm starting to fancy Manky Maureen".

Jonesy tossed a cigarette over to his mate chuckling. Manky Maureen, was the seventy something woman who took the money on the door and needed to wash under her arms more. Her hygiene, or lack of it, was one reason why people gave her a wide berth; the other was she reckoned she saw ghosts or 'the departed' as she called them.
"Oh come on," said Jonesy still laughing. "I think she's looking good tonight with that glitter on her hair, or it could be dandruff."
Both lads grinned and pulled with contentment on their smokes.

"Are you going to go up and do a bit of training when we have a break, Billy?
Cause these'll do you no good if you are. Well, they'll do you no good if you're not, according to me mam. Coffin nails she calls them. But I don't believe her," Jonesy mused looking at the glowing end of his cigarette. "I think she only says that so I'll stop and have more money to give her for me keep."

"Ya, I'm going up at break to do a bit," said Billy bouncing on his toes. "It's the boxing finals in a week or two and I want to be right at me peak. There's some good lads coming through so I'll have to get fit as a butcher's dog." He feinted a couple of punches, moving lightly on his feet as he moved around his imaginary opponent.

"Hey you look good enough to be a dancer on the stage prancing about like that Billy Mason; play your cards right and I just might let you have the last dance later." The voice belonged to Sadie Thompson and was as attractive as the rest of her.

For an answer Billy gave a long low wolf whistle as she drifted past him on a cloud of Chanel Number Five. He rolled his eyes upwards as he mouthed the word 'gorgeous' at Jonesy's grinning face.

The first part of the evening was lost in the comings and goings of the Saturday night crowd and Billy and the rest of the doormen were kept busy seeing everything ran as smoothly as the club management wanted. Break time came at last and Billy and Jonesy went up to the training room. The room was a space in the clock tower and both boys were panting a bit after running up the steep stairs which counted as part of their fitness regime. "Hey look here," puffed Billy excitedly as he burst into the room, "Fred Glynn's left that punch bag he promised us weeks ago." "It's seen better days," said Jonesy disdainfully, running his hand over the leather, "and this side of it looks ready to burst open any minute." "It'll do" was Billy's response. "It's summat for nothing and that's all right in my book. What we need now is a thick rope to hang it up with. Have a look in that big cupboard over there."

He nodded in the direction of a floor to ceiling cupboard which ran the length of the wall. "You know I never noticed this before." Jonesy was standing in front of the doors looking at how the cupboards tapered away to fit the arch in the ceiling. "Stop gawping at it and have a look if there's something in there we can use." "But I haven't seen it before honestly." Jonsey said, wondering how he had missed it. Manky Maureen appeared in the doorway.

"You wouldn't have noticed it before if the cupboard didn't

want you to," Maureen croaked as she cleared the phlegm from her throat. "You want to cut down on the fags, Maureen, that's a right cough you've got there," said Billy, as he fiddled about with the hook protruding from the ceiling. "and leave off with the mystics. Jonesy's likely to get frightened to death and shake all the change out of his pockets."

Both lads were still laughing when Jonesy pulled a long piece of rope out of the cupboard. "Hey look at this; it'll be great for hanging the bag on. Come on let's get it up there, Billy." Both of them were so involved in hanging the punch bag and making sure it was hanging right that they did not notice Maureen's expression as she watched what was going on. At last the bag was hanging straight and swinging in a perfect arc when punched. Billy, who had been standing on the ladder making last adjustments, turned round to acknowledge the congratulations he expected from Jonesy and Maureen."What's up with you two, you look like you've seen a ghost". Maureen and Jonesy were both staring at the bag. "What? What's up?" Billy looked at the bag, as it swung slowly backwards and forwards.

Just then the clock struck nine o'clock, the chimes echoing loudly in the small space. As the last note faded the bag dropped to the floor. "Oh bloody hell," said Billy going over to pick it up. "Don't touch it." shrieked Maureen, her voice making him jump. "Why what's up with it," asked Billy stepping backwards. Maureen pointed a shaking finger at the bag. "It's cursed that's what's up". "Don't talk so bloody daft woman, it's a punch bag, it fell down; I mustn't have fastened it tight enough. Tell her Jonesy." He looked across at his friend noticing his pale face and pointing finger. "What the hell's up with you? Don't let her put the wind up you, she's a nutter," said Billy cocking his thumb in Maureen's direction.

"I saw it Billy." Jonsey's voice was barely audible and his hands were shaking. "There was a man's body with a rope round his neck. He'd hanged himself and he were swinging slow. His face were horrible Billy." Jonsey sat down on the floor and covered his eyes, as though to blot out the images forced onto the back of his eyelids. "And when the clock stopped chiming, his body slumped on the rope, his head flopped to one side and his neck was all twisted. Then his tongue came out of the side of his mouth, He were dead Billy."

"What a load of bloody rubbish," roared Billy picking up the bag and lifting it up to re hang it from the hook in the beam.

"Its not rubbish Billy," croaked Maureen. "Caretaker, who worked here about sixty odd years ago, hanged himself from that hook. Story is his wife ran off with another bloke and he couldn't cope, couldn't get over it. That rope you've got out of that cupboard was what he used to hang himself with. Police brought it back when the inquest was over; I mean what you do with a rope that was used for that sort of a job?" she finished lamely, looking over at where it snaked harmlessly along the floor.

"I don't bloody believe it, Maureen, and what's more I'm rehanging this bag and I'm going to use it for me training," said Billy defiantly as he struggled up the ladder, the bag balanced on his shoulder. He looked down at Jonsey. "I don't know what you saw Jonsey, but I don't think it were what you said, I think it were a trick of the light, and then that clock started chiming, enough to scare the arse off anybody. Come on downstairs and get a drink, its gone cold up here. We could do with getting a heater or summat." The little trio clumped down the narrow stairs, all of then relieved to be away from the cold atmosphere of the clock room and back in the land of pulsating club music.

Billy was watching Jonesy closely as he gulped his tea down. "Listen, mate, let's keep it to ourselves what happened up there tonight. We don't want to be putting ideas into people's heads. Management will go effin' mad if trade falls off because of a bloody ghost story we started," said Billy giving a weak laugh. Jonesy put his cup down carefully and locked eyes with Billy. "Right, I'll go along with that. But I'm telling you one last time and I'll not mention it again, I saw summat Billy and I'm not going up there again for all the tea in China." He paused to let the moment lighten. "Or all the coffee in Brazil, or all the cocoa in wherever it comes from." Billy gave a relieved laugh and slapped his mate on the back. He was glad to clear away thoughts of ghosts and spooks between them and return to their normal joking around. "Fair enough, that's the end of it. Now come on, let's go and look at the talent of Oldham and the gorgeous Sadie," said Billy making his eye brows go up and down quickly, and at the same time pretending to wipe sweat off his face.

It was over a week before Billy could find time to go up to the clock room to have a training session and as he climbed the narrow stairs he was thinking about his training routine and which exercises he would do first. As he opened the door of the room he felt the drop in temperature."Eh it's bloody chilly in here. I'll have to get a heater in or summat." He soon forgot about the cold as his body warmed to the rhythm of his warm up exercises.

He worked consistently on each group of muscles, which once moving in harmony, would, he hoped, bring down his opponent at the boxing match next Saturday. For an hour the only sound to be heard was the steady thump, thump of flesh on leather, as Billy practiced his punches and moved lightly on his feet around the bag.

He was sweating hard now, his punches feeling smooth and accurate. "Eh that feels good," he thought as he stilled the bag so that it would not swing back and hit him as he towelled the sweat off himself. Ten minutes later the mechanism of the clock cranked itself up ready to strike the hour. Billy glanced at his watch, nine o clock. He pulled on the last of his clothes as the chimes began to ring out. Them clock mechanisms could do with some oil, they're creaking like mad he thought. He struggled to keep the sleeves of his jacket down as he pulled on his heavy overcoat. He felt the weight of a punch hit him in the small of his back, catching him unaware and nearly knocking him off balance. Turning round, he jumped out of the way as the punch bag swung slowly towards him, before the rope's momentum took it backwards again, all the time creaking loudly as it swung from the hook in the small space.

Billy was mesmerised, rooted to the spot. His heart was beating fast and fear gripped his stomach and dried his mouth. He became aware that it was colder in the room and he shivered. The chimes came to an end and the bag dropped to the floor. Billy ran out of the room, straight into manky Maureen. "Now do you believe there's summat up here?" she asked. "I've come up here every night since the last time the three of us were up here, and, at nine clock, the bag swings and drops to the floor after the last chime." She turned to Billy. But he was too busy taking the stairs two at a time and too far away to either hear her or or respond.

He was still in the grip of fear when he reached the club floor. He stood stock still allowing his brain to absorb the familiarity of the club scene. He looked back as the door to the clock tower opened and Maureen came through. She smiled at Billy."I'll ask you again lad. Now do you believe?" Billy studied her for a long moment before turning away and strolling back to his post on the door. "By heck it's cold tonight, Jonesy, have you got a fag to warm me hands on?" he asked quietly.

Authors note

The club in this story is Bailey's Nightclub at Star Inn, which used to be the Gaumont Cinema at one time. The young doorman, who I have called Billy is now in his fifties. He told me the story about the swinging punch bag in the small room behind the clock. The clock still looks down on Star Inn. So if you are passing any evening at nine clock, you may like to let your imagination wonder what is happening behind the silent brickwork. On the other hand, you may not wish to know.

Patricia Gray

THE FARM

"Are you ok, mister, are you lost or some 'at?"

The mousy-haired boy was about nine and small for his age. The man looked down at him, his smile wiping out the rather grim, sad expression that had disturbed the boy.

"Only lost in my memories, son, I used to live here when I was about your age."

"Huh," snorted the lad, "was it as scaggy then as it is now?"

"No. I lived on the farm."

"Farm!? What d'you mean? There's no farm round here. Not that I know of and I get everywhere."

"I bet you do," breathed the man.

He smiled again at the boy's suspicious glance.

"No, lad, it was long ago, before all the houses. There were fields as far as the eye could see. My granddad had forty acres and cows and a duck pond. I hardly know where I am now it's changed that much."

"Tell me about it."

"The farmhouse must have been where that spinney is now. It was a long stone house, low with narrow windows and big chimneys. Then there was a barn and cowshed and a cottage – a little house - where I lived with my mum and dad and my sister. Besides that there was the muck heap from when we cleaned out the cows and the horses - I fell in it once, I didn't half stink - and there was a well where we got our water. We pumped it up to a tap in the kitchen."

He paused to savour the memory.

"Go on, mister. Please."

The last word was added in response to a questioning look.

"We had a herd of cows, for the milk. Granddad had a milk round. We had horses to pull the cart. There weren't so many cars and vans in those days. We had a few goats and rabbits and chickens for the eggs and the meat. At the bottom of the slope there was a pond with ducks. I used to go fishing there with a little net. I only ever got sticklebacks and minnows – tiny little fish - and frog spawn in the spring, of course.

"The fields ran down to the railway line. There was a lane down that way between two high dry stone walls. Some of the fields were pasture where the animals went out to graze when it was warm enough and some were meadows where we let the grass grow long till the summer, then cut it and let it dry for hay and stored it in the barn for winter feed.

"The rabbits were in hutches near the barn and the chickens lived in the farmyard and round the house. My dad had a vegetable garden. He grew all sorts. We never had to buy any vegetables. There were fruit bushes, gooseberries and raspberries and some cherry trees and elder trees. My mum used to make wine from the elder flowers and elderberries. And she used to make jam from the cherries, those we didn't eat, and from the blackberries that grew in the hedges. Dad had a few beehives too, so we had honey. Lovely flavour it had, smelt of clover."

His voice faded away as reminiscence had him in its thrall.

"Did you play football, mister?"

"Only in school, at home I helped my granddad with the animals or I was in the garden with my dad or out in the fields with my friends. We used to dam the stream and build bridges over it. We built dens or we'd camp out in summer and have a bonfire with sausages. We had rope swings in the trees. In the winter, when it snowed, I'd get out the sledge my dad made and go sledging in the big meadow. It used to go that fast. But it was damp. I think I always wore wellies."

"Mind you, it was lovely and warm in the house, well in the kitchen. There was a range in the cottage and in the farmhouse. My mum and my gran did all the cooking on those, so the fire was always lit. They cooked stews with loads of dad's lovely veg and pies and cakes. My mouth's watering just to think of it. But in the winter the bedrooms were cold. You'd wake up in the morning and there'd be frost patterns down the window, on the inside. That was cold. And you had to wash in cold water too; it took too long to boil a kettle in the morning. But we had a bath every Friday, in the big, tin bath in front of the fire."

"Why did you stop living there?"

A curious expression, both sad and angry flitted over the man's face.

"One day a bloke came from the council. He said that the houses were unfit to live in what with there only being the well and no gas and no sewers. They condemned it and we all had to move out. Gran and granddad got a house nearby – they were just starting to build these houses then – so they

58

were able to carry on looking after the animals, but we were moved right up the hill. Then they compulsory purchased the land, said they needed it for the development plan. Granddad had no say; he only rented the farm. So that was that. We were out. And I've never been back from that day to this. And I'm not sure it was a good idea to come, but I wanted to see."

"But, mister, they never built nowt where your farm was. There's only trees over there."

"Yes, son, I know. Makes you think, doesn't it?"

Author's note

A friend told me of his sense of loss that he could never return to his grandfather's farm after the land was subject to a Compulsory Purchase Order shortly after the war. I have used some of his memories to set the scene and then imagined the activities.

Maggie Nicholson

I came out of the library looking at my watch. I felt cool, in every sense, in my cotton mini skirt and vest top. And the shrug was just right. I had to catch the bus at four thirty at the bus station by the Civic Centre but before that I needed to go to The Works and H&M in Spindles. I ran across the little garden, brilliant in the afternoon sunshine and up the steps to Union Street. I went through the gates to – nothing. The air was thick and a dirty greeny black. I remembered my gran telling me about fog and how you couldn't see your hand in front of you. I raised my hand; I couldn't see it.

I turned to the left anyway. After a few steps I came to the Post Office. Puddles of muddy golden light marked the high windows without illuminating the street. I could see the face of the big clock, but strangely I could not read the time on it. An old lady wearing a thick coat and a head scarf tied under her chin was buying stamps at the machine. The copper surround of the letter slot gleamed even in the gloom and I could read 'POSTING BOX' in white capitals quite clearly.

"How do, Mrs. Enright."

A bandy legged little man loomed into view, raised his cap politely and disappeared again before I could catch the reply. I crossed Greaves Street gingerly, though there seemed to be little traffic.

The Lyceum across the road was invisible and from the road I heard the clip-clop of horses' hooves on the cobblestones and a hoarse voice calling indistinguishably. That would be Mr Hickey, the rag-tatter, who lived just round the corner. No one would be coming out with old stuff or wanting a donkey stone this weather.

I walked past the Baths; again the light was visible but cheerless. A group of schoolboys plunged out of the door in an odour of hot water and soap. They each carried a damp towel rolled under an arm. They wore caps and short trousers with tweed jackets and long grey knee socks and lace-up shoes. I smiled to see that every one of them had a sock that was concertinaing gently towards the ankle; then I winced at the angry, red chap lines where rough, woollen trousers had chafed their skin and the scabs on their knees from where they had fallen. I thought I heard, "sir said" but within less than a minute they had disappeared into the blinding murk.

I trudged on, passing a few little shops and the electricity show room. I paused gratefully in the entrance to take stock. A group of men walked past wearing flat caps and with long scarves wrapped round the lower part of their faces.

"You'll never believe it," one said, "they wanted half a crown for that rubbish."

"Aye," said another, "Prices are going daft. My bus fare from Hill Stores was tuppence ha'penny and even the kiddies have to pay three ha'pence."

I shook my head trying to understand what had been said. The fog swirled and hid them from view.

The pub was dark; well it was half past three. As I crossed Hobson Street; a group of girls giggled past me, talking loudly, and leading one of their number, who was twined in coloured ribbons. I knew then it was Friday and she was getting married the next day.

Then it was the Nelson. I carried on, not seeing the church

behind its low wall with the scars of the absent railings; after that there was more welcome light from the billiard hall. A bus drew up at the stop; the platform at the back was crowded with people waiting to get off. As they did the conductor called something that I didn't quite catch. It must have been funny as everybody laughed and someone called back, but again I had the feeling that I had misheard everything.

It would be the doctor's next, then Brunswick Street. There was the familiar acrid reek of the blacksmith's at the next corner, noticeable even over the sooty smell of the fog, and the impatient whinny of a waiting horse. The little sweet shop on the corner tempted me to go in and get some Victory Vs, but somehow I couldn't open the door.

A few more shops came and went. Three older ladies plodded past. I glanced curiously at them. Two wore heavy coats and had headscarves over curlers in their hair. The third had a dull shawl over her head and shoulders and safety-pinned under her chin. All had odd little wisps of cotton sticking to their clothes and talked in strange, cracked voices. All seemed deathly tired. They didn't seem to notice me any more than the other people I had seen.

The aroma of spiced meat tantalised my nostrils. Should I stop at Horsman's for a dinky pie? I hesitated then went on, past the flower shop, across Chaucer Street, dodging a Post Office van going to the sorting office. I edged carefully round the railings to avoid falling down the steps to the underground toilets in front of the Gaumont. I wrinkled my noise at the whiff that came out.

I went up to shelter under the cinema's lighted canopy. What was on? The Absent- minded Professor with Fred

McMurray; that should be funny. The second film was The Horsemasters. I might go tomorrow night.

I went towards the crossing to George Street. That was easy. Every corner of the Star Inn crossroads was lit by a naphtha flare. I crossed and stepped into George Street. The fog lifted. I looked back along the sunlit street, back into 2009.

Author's note

I recall vividly struggling home through 'peasoupers'. To this I have added other snippets of memory, both my own and other people's, plus little bits of family history.

Peggy Bottomley

FRIENDSHIP EXPOSED

My Friday began around 4am, and thereafter continued to deteriorate. In fact not a minute of the day was agreeable.

To begin with the temperature was sub-zero and the damned van wouldn't start. After struggling to locate the fault with my scant knowledge of mechanics, I resorted to threatening it with a one-way trip to the scrap yard. Apparently surrendering, the van reluctantly conceded to fire up. I finally left home 40 minutes late in a foul temper.

I picked up Splat; he was shivering violently and extremely hacked off at my tardiness. He expressed his displeasure at length, punctuating his speech with abundant profanities, which he knows I find distasteful. I was tempted to forcefully eject him from the van, and enjoyed a fleeting mental image of my boot mark on his skinny posterior. Suppressing this idea with some regret, I inserted a John Denver CD and turned up the volume. Splat loathes my taste in music.

In case you were wondering, Splat acquired his nickname when some careless idiot accidentally upended a gallon of white gloss paint from a first storey windowsill. Little Jock, as he was known until that instant, happened to be standing directly underneath. The perpetrator of the accident, yours truly, was also re-named in honour of the occasion. 'Don't ask! Just call me Mick'.

To continue; late start, freezing weather, fog, blocked motorway, wrong parts, forgotten tools, bad organisation on site, Splat sulking ... I won't bore you with the details!

Around 8pm, tired, hungry, and irritable I was forced to give in and accept that we would need to stay overnight, which destroyed my plans for the weekend and vexed me even further. To pile on the suffering, we spent a fruitless couple of hours in search of accommodation. Apparently there was a Conservative party annual conference taking place over the weekend, it would have been a small measure of comfort had it been a Labour conference.

Splat's continuous carping about having to work the weekend was most unwelcome at this point, I ordered him to be quiet - very impolitely. By the time we approached the next guesthouse I was prepared to kill. In contrast to the low garden walls surrounding the neighbouring buildings, a high solid wooden fence we can barely see over surrounded this one. Attached to the gate was a shabby sign marked 'accommodation.' An arrow pointed to a buzzer. I pushed it.

The gate opened with a spine-chilling creak. Behind it stood a squat, obese person dressed in dirty, food-stained clothes. His pale sweaty face was a very unhealthy colour, and the stringy remnants of his long greasy grey hair hung to his shoulders either side of his baldhead. He coldly observed us with jaundiced eyes. The entrance hall exuded a disagreeable odour of cat, cooked cabbage and God knows what else.

'Er,' I began uncertainly, revolted by his appearance, 'Do you have rooms available?'

'£50 each. No breakfast,' he informed us in a cold tone that effectively discouraged any negotiation.

'Could we see the rooms please?'

Without uttering a word, he showed us two adjacent double rooms, my house-proud mother would have collapsed at the sight of them.

'Where's the bathroom?' I demanded.

By way of reply he pointed to a door at the end of the corridor and went back downstairs, leaving us to follow.

'Just tonight!' I proffered my credit card. Judging by his expression, it was about as acceptable as a bar of soap.

'Cheque?' I asked hopefully.

'Cash. In advance.'

Fortunately, we just managed to scrape the cash together between the two of us. To be precise I ended up in debt to Splat to the tune of £45.37, which prompted him to give vent to another stream of complaints. The proprietor accepted our payment without thanks and provided our door keys with some verbal instructions. 'The doors are equipped with automatic closers. Don't leave your room without taking your key. If you lock yourself out, push the intercom at the gate. I don't like being woken up in the middle of the night.' He departed without further comment – probably to underneath his favourite stone.

We fetched our belongings from the van. I entered my room, unpacked my towel, (none were provided) and with key in hand I headed for the bathroom. The toilet was crusted with brown stains; there was no seat and no toilet paper. Having waited in vain for the water to heat, I balefully regarded the dirty washbasin and decided not to bother.

Too tired to go out and eat, I wolfed down a sandwich, left over from lunchtime and fell exhausted into the bed.

Some time later I woke up needing the bathroom.

Sleepily, eyes half shut, I groped my way in the dark. I was in midstream when I heard the door slam. My heart sank faster than a leaking, lead filled boat.

Having completed the necessities, I stood outside my door and hopelessly willed it to open whilst considering my options. Waking up Splat and asking to share his bed was a little tricky, I was stark naked. I gloomily descended the stairs, went outside and hobbled to the gate, the gravel cutting painfully into my bare feet.

'Oh hell,' I cursed, realising I needed to go into the street to reach the intercom button. I considered again waking up Splat. He hadn't forgiven me for the paint spill episode and would relish an opportunity to reap his revenge by spreading the story of my mishap, no doubt exaggerating all the details to embarrass me to the maximum.

Opting for the lesser of the two evils, I opened the gate and peeked out; there were several clubs and bars on the street, and unfortunately a large number of people walking between them.

Steeling my nerves and playing it cool, I stepped into the street, nonchalantly walked up to the intercom and pressed the buzzer continuously, ignoring the laughter, catcalls, whistles, vulgar comments and propositions. A grunt informed me my host was awake, I reentered the garden and gratefully shut the gate, but not before I had taken my ovation with an appropriate gesture – borrowed from a certain jockey named Mr Smith.

Back indoors, shivering with cold, I fearfully watched my rescuer approaching slowly up the stairs. On arrival, he stared at me for a long moment his expression unreadable.

Then his lip curled upwards into a sinister sneer. It sudden-ly occurred to me how he might interpret the situation, as he gazed at me standing before him, naked and trembling.

He unlocked the door of my room and opened it. I brushed passed him swiftly, without expressing my gratitude and pushed hard against the door, closing it noisily against him.

Breathing heavily with relief and trying not to inhale the lingering smell of his rancid body odour, I listened atten-tively to his progress back down the stairs, and didn't re-lax until I was certain he had gone. It took me a while to calm down and fall asleep again. But not for long ......

I felt a movement on the bed. Greasy hair brushing my cold skin. My eyes snapped open in terror. One hand was almost touching me, the other tapping a rhythm on the bedside table.

'Stop!' I yelled fearfully.

He stopped tapping and moved closer. The knock-ing continued loudly. Grinning evilly, he waved both hands in the air mockingly, then lunged.

Yelling in terror, I dived sideways out of the bed and land-ed heavily on the floor.

'Mick, open the door.'

My senses reeling I staggered to my feet, the knocking still pounding in my head.

'Mick! For Pete's sake! Wake up!'

'Splat?' Groggily, I pulled on my jockey shorts, turned on

the light and opened the door.

Splat, so skinny he appeared to be on the verge of starvation, and blessed with a pimply face only a mother could love, was clad in a pair of well-washed baggy underpants. Still in a state of shock, I stared at him bewildered.

'I've been knocking on this door for ages Mick. Look, I know this looks bad, but I'm locked out. I went for a pee and the bloody door shut.'

I continued to stare, trying to pull myself together.

'For God's sake Mick! Say something! Let me in.'

I opened the door wider not trusting myself to speak.

'Look mate, I'm really sorry. I feel so embarrassed. I didn't dare to knock up the landlord, he gives me the creeps.'

My nerves still rattled, I had nonetheless recovered sufficiently to recognise the advantage to be gained from this fortunate turn of events. I blatantly exploited the situation.

'I wouldn't be daft enough to lock myself out Splat, but if I had done so, I would have preferred to wake up the proprietor.'

'You would?'

'Splat, if I had appeared at your door, clad in my y fronts, at some God forsaken hour of the night, wanting to share your bed, you would revel in telling everyone we know.'

'Yeah I sure would,' he grinned happily at the thought.

Realization dawned. The grin faded rapidly and he back-pedalled at the speed of light.

'No! No mate! No! I swear! No! I wouldn't have said a word!'

I climbed into bed.

'You may as well get in Splat, your chastity is in no danger,' I said, turning my back to him.

'Please mate! Don't say a word about this. The lads are still ribbing me about the paint incident'. He sounded close to tears.

'Goodnight Splat.'

I looked at my watch before turning off the light.

It was 4am. Anticipating the jokes I would share tomorrow at poor Splat's expense, I had a smile on my face for the first time in 24 hours.

Author's Note:

This story is based on a real occurrence, which happened to my husband several years ago when he was working away from home.

The true facts, as told in the story, are as follows:

Whilst staying in lodgings and following a trip to the bathroom, my husband unfortunately became locked out of his room in the middle of the night, in a state of complete nakedness. He had a choice of two options: disturbing his co-

worker, asleep in the next room to his, or venturing outside the premises into the street in order to ring the doorbell and awaken the proprietor. The option he opted for in the story is also factual.

The rest of this tale and the characters are products of my imagination, employed to create this humorous short story, which is probably my personal favourite. I hope you like it too.

Lesley Truchet

THE GATES

"So you got your way then?"

The grating voice interrupted Lydia's train of thought. She'd been admiring the alley gates that blocked off the backs; they had nagged the council for so long to get them.

"Well, it's for everybody's benefit, Mr. Ackroyd. You know those kids on the motorbikes have been driving us all mad and all those wagging it from school and smoking and leaving all their mess in the back. And what about those break-ins?"

"And what about all the rubbish and junk that's been dumped here? Not thought about that, have you? Who's responsible for clearing it all up? You've landed us with a right burden here."

"He's got a point, you know."

Lydia had recounted this further example of awkwardness over tea. Gary, her husband considered carefully before carrying on.

"There is a load of junk and I bet the council won't want to know, so it will be down to us."
Lydia phoned Marie, Pete and Steve who ran the local home watch groups.

The following evening saw them and a group of neighbours inspecting the back soberly. Unusually it was made up of three branches off a wide central triangle with houses from three streets backing on to it.

"It could be brilliant," said Steve in a depressed tone.

"But it is a right mess," added Marie.

They walked up and down surveying the stacks of old tyres, the broken pallets, the bike wheels, the squashed cans, plastic bottles, fag packets and the revolting, stinking piles of dog mess. There were branches of trees torn down and rampant weeds against the walls.

On the plus side there were several trees, climbers were peeping over from backyards, some people had planted clumps of flowers outside their own back gates and there was quite a bit of grass.

"Suppose," said Gary, "we collected it all into the triangle part and then sorted it out. At least we'd have all the mess in one place and we'd see a bit more clearly."

"Yes we'd have a big pile of c…"

"I know Steve," Gary broke in, "but we can put the bottles, cans and paper in the recycling bins that aren't full the night before they empty the bins. We can do the same with the stuff you can't recycle. The pallets have a phone number on them, so we can get someone to come and pick them up."

"That leaves us with the tyres and the doggy dos and the things that won't go in the bin."

"If we pile up a few tyres we can shovel up the poo and dump it in. if we put in that soil from the far end, in layers it will compost down."

The next weekend was overcast, so nobody really minded putting in a stint of back clearing. Gary was ruefully amused when Steve piled up four tyres and then handed him a shovel. Pete barrowed in the soil and everyone else set about picking litter into carrier bags and moving the more unwieldy items. Five o'clock on Sunday saw the whole neighbourhood filthy, exhausted, but triumphant drinking tea, beer or orange juice and munching the cakes and biscuits that Mrs. O'Neill and Miss Travis, two cheerful ladies in their eighties, had baked.

Slowly, painfully slowly, over the next three weeks they got rid of the rubbish that was relatively easy to deal with.

"What now?" Steve sounded exhausted.

The five others who had worked in the back that weekend looked despairingly at the collection of junk that still cluttered up the triangle.

"If we pile up all the tyres like that first lot," offered Gary, "we can use them as planters. If we put in things that hang down they'll hide the tyres."

"What about the expense?"

"I've got the old grow bags from my tomatoes and other people may have too," Pete suggested.

"And we can ask Alan Crowther if he has any ideas. He has an allotment and he did a great job tidying up the trees and getting the weeds out."

"Right, Gary, but he also left us the job of getting rid of all that."

"I think we should have a bonfire party." Lydia had arrived unnoticed with cans of beer. "We can use it to get

shot of other junk too."
The men looked at her in amazement.

"Why didn't I think of that?" laughed Gary.

Half term came. Jimmy, Lydia and Gary's son and his friend Paul, son of Pete mooched disconsolately up and down the back. Their mums had told them that no, they were not going to have a laugh in Town Square with the bigger boys and they were fed up with playing football on their own. Jimmy kicked savagely at the pile of wood and other combustibles stacked up for the bonfire.

"Hey, you'll have that down, and your mothers'll give you what for if you scuff your shoes."
Mr. Ackroyd wore his normal scowl.

"It's not fair. We're not allowed to do anything."

"When I was your age I'd have used some of that stuff to build a bogey."

"What d'you mean?"

The old man explained. He drew a plan in the dirt with a stick. He directed them as they gathered what they needed from the pile of junk, and then he went for his tool box.

When Lydia went out to call the two boys for their meal she found the three of them carefully assembling the front axle.

"It's great, mum, Bill's showing us how to build a bogey and we can play with it and use it to help move things." Jimmy was almost stuttering with excitement.

"Mr Ackroyd, don't you mean?"

"It's all right, missus, I told them to call me Bill. They're a pair of really good lads. We've got on great."

"Well, I'm Lydia. Will you come in and have a bite to eat with us. It's only bacon and egg. Then you two boys will have to get washed and changed. The boss said you can come into work with me today as it's only an hour till your dads get home."

"Oh mum, that's gross. We've a load to do here."

"Well you can't stay at home on your own – and it was very good of Mr Brown. Not many bosses would do that."

"Lydia, if you trust me they can stay and we can finish the bogey off."

Lydia looked in amazement at her neighbour. He flushed slightly.

"I know I'm a bit crabby sometimes. But I've really enjoyed the boys' company. I feel ten years younger.

It was the fifth of November. Virtually everyone was gathered round. The bonfire was well ablaze; the first rocket shot up. Decorators' tables stood against the walls laden with potatoes wrapped in foil to bake in the embers later, with sausages on long sticks, with Miss Travis' best parkin and the ginger beer that Mrs O'Neill had got all the kids brewing. She'd also brought some sarsaparilla and dandelion and burdock she'd made herself.

"I'll show you how to do that too," she'd assured Maisie, a nervous fifteen year old who thought that the old drinks would make a good part of her GCSE project. "Mr Benson used to have a herb beer shop across the road and I used to help Saturday. He showed me how to make the drinks."

"Cool," said Maisie with eyes shining. She adored Mrs O'Neill who was so patient showing her how to make things and never laughed at her for being a bit slow.

"Great night the other day."

Steve was amazed when the bloke from the end house, who drove a Merc and never had anything to say to anyone, stopped him on the way out of the paper shop.

"Yes, it was, wasn't it? Mind you, once Bill Ackroyd started pulling out any useful wood I'm amazed we had anything left to burn. Oh I'm Steve Walsh by the way."

"Oh, the Home Watch chap. Sorry I can't be more involved, but I'm out a lot. I'm David Ellis. My wife's Susie."

The two men shook hands and chatted briefly.

"You haven't thought of having a carol concert, have you? I've noticed that there are quite a few oldies. I bet they'd love it."

"That's a good idea. We were wondering what to do next?"

It was freezing cold when they finished with 'God Rest You Merry Gentlemen' so they were all glad to get into David and Susie's. Their living room – they'd had the internal walls knocked down to suit open-plan living and then added a conservatory – was the only space indoors big enough to hold everyone. Everyone had brought a mug as instructed and the group of ladies who had nipped in during the last carol to be ready dished out hot chocolate, tea, and mulled wine. A jug of coffee and another of orange juice and a few cans of beer were handy on the island unit. Maisie was practically bursting with pride as she handed round the mince pies. Mrs O'Neill and Miss Travis assured her that she was turning into a very good cook and that her help was invaluable and she was now a firm member of the local cooking circle.

For the ladies and Mr Greene, who had been on his own since his wife died, had started a little cooking service for those who needed it. They were paid in 'gates' the currency for these exchanges. Other people did babysitting, Bill Ackroyd did odd jobs and woodwork, and some others helped with furniture moving or heavy cleaning, or walked dogs or gave lifts. Even the teenagers loved it because they could do something and receive a tangible reward. A couple of hours spent babysitting for the Eliots, for example, could allow you to ask Miss Travis for one of her mouth-watering cheese and onion pies.

"Well the next event is the trip to the panto in the New Year. All the kids are going I think. What shall we do after that? In any case Happy Christmas everyone." Steve's announcement came as the party broke up and everyone went home in a flurry of good wishes.

On the 15th of January it snowed heavily. Even the main road was solid; no buses passed and the bitter wind whipped the faces of anyone daring to step out. On the sixteenth the sun shone coldly on the pristine white. By the afternoon the imprisoned mums were only too glad to let their restless children, deprived of school by the weather, go and play in the back where they could enjoy the snow in safety.

"We'll certainly beat you lot," crowed Barry Jones.

This was followed by prolonged calling, giggling and the steady thump of snowballs against walls, fences and the gates to the back yards.

"It's such a relief," Lydia sighed to Marie over a cup of coffee. The bigger ones are being great with the little kids and at least with the gates locked they're all safe."

Hardly had she finished speaking than there was the crash of breaking glass and a man's angry shout. The two women charged out to find the children scattering in all directions and Dave Ellis, incandescent with rage, beside his Mercedes with the windscreen shattered. He'd driven in, carefully, to put the car in the carport that took up half his back yard when a snowball with a stone inside had smashed into the car. He was inconsolable.

"I'll put a stop to all this nonsense," he snarled, rejecting Marie's efforts to calm him down.

The atmosphere for the next few days was dreadful. Nobody was blaming anyone out loud, but many people were regretting the breach to the neighbourly cooperation caused by a few seconds of adolescent foolishness.

"It can't go on," murmured Steve when he and Pete met in Marie's house, "we've all too much to lose."

"But Dave won't listen to anyone," put in Marie. "He's still furious and you can't blame him."

"I've had a bit of an idea," said Pete. "I need to do some checking, and then Marie, you'll need to tackle Susie and we'll all need to go and see the parents of the kids who were snowballing."

"You were brilliant," Lydia told her friend two weeks later.

"Oh, it was Pete's idea. He found out about the excess for a windscreen. We all went to see the parents to ask them to contribute and I got Susie to talk Dave round. A bit of good came out of it too. Young Barry went down to apologise and got to talking cars and to cut a long story short Dave's got him a Saturday job at his brother's garage. Barry's made up because he wants to be a mechanic and his mum's thrilled because she's had a bit of a struggle since her Al died last year."

"You know, Mr. Ackroyd, I know we were silly putting stones in the snowballs and causing all the fuss, but I can't really be sorry because so much good has come out of it."

"Like your job, you mean?"

"Well there is that. Mr. Ellis was great about mentioning me to his brother, but there are other things too. It's like everybody got a bit of a scare and realised how much better everything is now and we don't want to lose it."

Bill Ackroyd grunted encouragingly, thinking of the last couple of years when Barry and his friends had been wild and noisy and irritated all the neighbours. It was true. They had all been more responsible and helpful recently.

"I expect you've noticed everybody seems to be doing their bit to make things nicer. When Mrs Smith's mum died she brought the benches from her garden and put them over there." Barry pointed. "And other people have put seats out. The trees that Mr. Crowther pruned look lovely; and he's planted some fruit trees along the wall; and loads of people have put bulbs and other plants into those stacks of tyres and some other pots and stuff. It looks great."

The older man looked at Barry's shaggy, shoulder length mane, his t-shirt with a slogan bordering on indecency and his carefully ripped jeans and thought he'd never heard a teenager so articulate. But then again, he'd never really wanted to listen. The lads had been so annoying all he'd wanted was for them to shut up and go away.

"Call me Bill, lad," he surprised himself by saying. "All the little'uns do and to be straight with you 'Mr. Ackroyd' was a right grumpy old beggar."

"Ok, Bill, thanks," grinned Barry, blushing slightly, "mind you, to be straight with you, we gave you a lot to be grumpy about."

Bill's face suddenly took on a curious expression, half sheepish, half sly.

"To tell you the truth you lot didn't get up to the half of what me and my mates did. Come in and I'll brew up. I bet I'll surprise you."

"Honestly the stories Bill Ackroyd's been telling the kids! I'll kill him if any of them try any of his tricks."

"What those lads got up to was nobody's business. I remember when the whole gang of them set fire to old Mr Jones' hen pen when he gave it up. That'd be your Al's granddad. Well he'd said they could have it for a bonfire, but instead of waiting for November 5th they set fire to it right away, silly beggars. My brother, Tom was one of them. We had the police round. My mother was that ashamed. My father took a slipper to his backside." Miss Travis laughed. "He had to eat his tea standing up. Rest him."

"Well Barry came back with a tale about them using steel rope to slide down like on an assault course over on the ash pits where the old mill used to be. And he'd no more sense than to tell Joe, who told all his mates and now they're forever asking, "Can we go round to Bill's" and "Tell us about when you were a little boy, Bill"

"But he's a lot pleasanter for it. Very nice and helpful now."

It was a sunny Sunday afternoon in late May. The trees that Alan had pruned so carefully were in flower; the cherry blossom was almost over but there were fragrant curds of elderflower and rowan scenting the air. Raspberry canes and gooseberries were flourishing here and there along the walls. Bird feeders hung from branches and there was a birdbath and some of the group were getting quite expert at identifying feathered visitors. The stacks of tyres were blooming with bulbs and primulas; tulips were gently framed by forget-me-nots. Strawberry runners were spilling down the sides with very promising flowers.

Mrs O'Neill and Miss Travis were settled on the bench with mugs of tea, a box of biscuits and their knitting. Round them was a rough circle of camping chairs, deck chairs and plastic garden chairs as more and more of the women had come out to join them.

Maisie was learning to knit too now. Lydia had finished her housework for the week and told herself she deserved a break before tackling the ironing. Susie Ellis and Marie, had seen the others and come to join them bringing Brenda Jones with them. And the group had been growing slowly ever since. It was often like this now, thought Lydia, when it was fine. She thought back to the previous year when Gary had been working away so much and she'd been so lonely. That certainly wasn't a problem now. She sighed and reached for another home made ginger nut.

Over the wall Bill Ackroyd's voice made itself heard.

"Did I ever tell you about that trick we had with the door knockers?"

"No, Bill, go on," came a chorus of small boys.

"Well we looped a long washing line through all the door knockers, and then knocked at one house. When they opened the door, and closed it when they saw nobody there, it made all the other door knockers knock. So everybody else came to the door and all the knockers kept knocking. Nobody could open the door wide enough to get out. Somebody had to come from round the back. We didn't get caught doing that either."

Muffled giggles were enough to make all the listening women decide to put their washing lines away carefully.

"We did have another trick with doors," continued Bill. "We'd stick a drawing pin onto the thumb latch with a bit of horse muck – Mr Dawson the carter had his stable just round the corner – folk would press down to open the door, prick their thumb and then lick it – it's the normal thing to do. You should have seen their faces!"

"Mummy, that is so gross," said Debbie Ellis from

where the little girls had been playing quietly unnoticed.

"It's a good thing we don't have thumb latches anymore," laughed Marie.

"Have you seen this?" asked Susie, indicating her Sunday paper.

Lydia leaned across to look and proceeded to read snippets of the article out loud.

'Get to know your neighbours. Lunch together on 19th July and help to rebuild your neighbourhood.'

"Well we've started already, but that shouldn't stop us. What do you think?"

The morning of 19th July was fine and sunny. Suddenly everyone was busy. Decorators' tables were placed securely round the edges of the Triangle; chairs were brought out and conservatory furniture. Later some of the men set up gazebos, sun umbrellas, card tables and camping tables. Barry organised the older kids to cover the tables with paper table cloths then place the paper plates, napkins and plastic cutlery. Towards twelve Dave Ellis started to set up the bar with wine, beer, soft drinks, water and jugs of sangria.

Later still people brought out their contributions to the feast and placed it under Miss Travis' eagle eye – varieties of salads, plates of cold meat, pies, quiches, bread and butter, cheese. Further away was the sweet table with trifles and cakes, cheesecake and mousse. Three different men had set up barbecues in their own back yards, one grilling fish, another chicken and chops and the third sausages and burgers.

And nobody needed an invitation. There may have been a little good-natured jostling, but the succulent aromas drew people to the food. "It reminds me," said Bill Ackroyd, "of the party they had for the kids for the Coronation. It was in the old barn. Such plates of sandwiches! Trays of jellies! Pyramids of cakes! There was a little girl next to me, about five, I suppose, and her eyes were out on stalks. Well none of us had seen anything like it with the rationing. She had her eye on a mini Swiss roll wrapped in silver paper – and so had I. And I snaffled it. There were loads. I got them all. I was a little pig in them days. Hey, Lydia, can I have another helping of trifle."

Author's note

I was inspired by the ideas of the potential for the regeneration of community behind the protection of the alley gates. To this I added snippets of memory, both my own and those of other people, and awareness of the unsung talents of retired people. Then I imagined how this might come together for everyone's benefit.

Maggie Nicholson

THE HOLLINWOOD DRAGON

"Please, Mr!"

Johnny Thornton thought himself made of feathers; his puny frame made no difference to the whacks Mr. Middleton's huge hand delivered to his little sister's backside. He dangled from the angry man's coat sleeve, and added a few kicks to Mr. Middleton's shins each time he was lifted in the wake of the relentless onslaught.

"Please, she doesn't know any better," Johnny tried again, and this time, the older man's arm bent to the plea. Johnny's sister was released.

Knowing better than to look a gift horse in the mouth, Ann un-wobbled her jellied legs and cowered behind Johnny. Mr. Middleton was red in the face—whether from exertion or anger, Johnny couldn't tell, but he spoke in a level and controlled manner when he looked Johnny square in the eye and said, "You better make sure she starts to know better. She's lucky to be alive." He gestured toward the smouldering bonfire. It spat out a riot of orange sparks with all the ambition of a would-be volcano.

"I will. Promise." Johnny backed into Ann, who took it as a cue to make a swift exit. Both children ran out of S. Margaret's churchyard and down Chapel Road.

They didn't stop until they reached the other side of the lake and the church was hidden from view by the cottages. Ann was trying not to cry. She was very brave for a seven year-old. Johnny doubted many of the younger lads in the gang could put up with the beating she'd had and not wail like a baby. He offered her a piece of liquorice he was saving in his pocket. She took it and tried a smile.

"What don't I know, Johnny?"

"A lot, I'll bet."

"No, I mean what Mr. Middleton said—you have to tell me. I did as you said. I didn't do it wrong."

A flash of frustration flared in Johnny's eyes. Ann knew it was time to be quiet. She sucked the liquorice and tested the tenderness of her bottom by sitting on the cobbles. Johnny sat down next to her, and sighed. "Yes, you did alright, but you chose the wrong bonty. No one takes wood from S. Margaret's bonfire."

"Why? If it's alright to raid Washbrook's and S. Thomas's, why not that one? It's the best there is—there's even a railway sleeper on it. I've never seen anyone guarding it, and you can't count Mr. Middleton as a guard, because he's an old man."

Johnny shuffled closer to his sister. "That bonfire doesn't need a gang of kids guarding it. It's got a dragon." Ann forgot her injuries altogether and laughed out loud. The look on Johnny's face silenced her. He continued, "You could have fallen in. Didn't you see it was lighted?"

"Of course I saw it was lighted, but that big sleeper was hardly scorched. I thought I could get at it."

Johnny lost all patience with his tiny ward. He stood up and kicked dust over the soggy end of her liquorice. "Well, you thought wrong, and the Hollinwood Dragon nearly gobbled you up."

are you going? Mum told you not to leave me."

"I'm going cob-coaling. Are you coming?"

Ann stood up sharp, tucked the dusty black sweet in her pocket and fell into step with Johnny. They walked back up Hollins Road and Johnny pointed out the good houses for them to call at.

"We'll try this one, because the man works at the paper mill and he might have all sorts of stuff for our bonty."

They knocked, and the pinch-faced woman who answered the door let them get all the way to the end of the cob-coaling song before she tutted and closed the door on them. Ann was outraged. She'd learned all the words. They had better luck a few houses down, where a new couple had moved in and wanted to get rid of the pigeon coop in the back yard. Both children were so overloaded with wood that they made their way straight to the plot where their own bonfire was steadily growing in size. Tomorrow it would be November 5th and their bonty would be the talk of the Parish.

They stacked all the wood, except for the coop, inside the shelter Jimmy Cardiff had made as a hiding place. Johnny thought it a shame to break up the coop. It was rotten in a few places, but could easily be patched up to house their father's chicks next year. They made their way home with it—Ann at the rear and Johnny up front—past the coal-sooted window frames of the terraces. A blanket of evening smog began to soup around them.

"Tell me now, Johnny," Ann continued to ruminate, "why S. Margaret's are allowed a bonty in the churchyard, when all the the other churches aren't."

"Because there really is a dragon asleep under it, and if a fire isn't lit on November fifth, it gets out and eats everyone. Haven't you seen all those dragons carved into the pews, and in the banners, and on the iron gates? They're all over the church."

Ann dropped her side of the coop. One wet corner struck the paving slab with a splintered slap.

Johnny was about to shout at her, but one look at her pale face and trembling lip forewarned him of a possible telling off at home. "Give over, Ann. We'll never get back at this rate."

"Tell me the truth—is there a dragon?"

"Why else do you think there are miners down the pits, and filthy, great, belching chimneys with smoke coming out of them? They're looking for the hoard. Everyone knows that dragons sit on piles of jewels and gold. The Hollinwood dragon sleeps on top of the Hollinwood treasure. That's a fact. Ask anyone." Ann did not look comforted, so Johnny continued. "It won't get you, if the Parish Priest lights a bonty tomorrow night, the dragon will think that it's still happy and safe in hell, so it will stay there."

"And if he doesn't?" Ann prodded.

Johnny turned, gleaming teeth grinning in delighted horror. "Then I wouldn't want to be a virgin maid."

Ann wrinkled her nose in thought, "What's a virgin?"

Johnny laughed. "It's a girl with a blue headscarf who hasn't got a cot for her baby so the poor thing has to sleep with the animals."

Ann looked down at the old pigeon coop. "I haven't got a blue headscarf, and I'm not putting my dolly in this smelly old thing."

"Then you're probably not a virgin, so I wouldn't worry about the dragon waking up."

Ann seemed satisfied with this. She picked up her end of the coop and the two lugged it home through the fog.

They reached the warmth of home just as the first, fat drop of rain smeared the soot on the kitchen window-sill. Within five minutes, the fog dissipated under the on-slaught of a horrendous autumnal storm. Johnny and Ann watched the lightning fork with excited eyes. In the mo-ments between strikes, thunder added a kettle-drum rum-ble to the steady percussion of persistent rain that raced down the window pane. The temperature waged a war for the house; heat prickled their backs from the glowing coals of the fireplace, while goosebumps chilled their fore-arms leaning on the sill, leaving them mottled mockeries of porcelain white in the glare of each flash of lightning. As the two children watched the battle rage, the scent of bacon and egg cast a spell on their hungry tummies, but it still took a lot of effort for them to ignore the spec-tacle of nature's light show and have a wash before tea.

Their father came through the door as mum was serving up. He put his tool bag on the table next to the frying pan and kissed his wife on the cheek.

Mrs Thornton batted him away from her. "Get that bag off the table before Johnny starts rummaging, and go have a proper wash—you're getting coal dust everywhere, including me."

Mr Thornton did as he was told, and shot Johnny a warning look as he stowed his tools on a shelf in the pantry. "Mind what your mother said. I had to borrow Jim Wakefield's good hammer today, because mine had wandered off with you."

Even though he washed at the colliery, and again in the basin, the rain had found enough bare skin on Brian Thornton to daub him with grey patches. Ann studied him as he ate. Black pin-pricks pocked his arms and neck. "Did the dragon bite you, daddy?" she asked.

Mr Thornton looked up at Ann from his dinner plate with a raised eyebrow. He settled his glance on Johnny. "Have you been filling her head with dragons and daftness?"

Johnny could feel the heat of his cheeks reddening. "I only told her about the Hollinwood dragon."

Mr Thornton nodded, and with a serious expression, turned to Ann. "Yes, you could say that I've been bitten by the dragon. It eats all the sheep on the hills, shits out coal, and then it's my job to clean up after it."

"Brian!" Johnny's mother had brought her own plate to the table, and nearly dropped it when her husband swore.

"Sorry, love. Bad day. Forget it, eh?"

Mrs Thornton put on a good show of pious outrage and then gave into a smile. The family ate and shared stories of their day, while the cacophony of the elements outside continued unheeded.

By the morning, last night's storm had been reduced to an embarrassed light drizzle. The children dressed for the Sunday Parish Mass, with strict instructions to stay away from muddy puddles. They took their usual seats alongside the Wakefield family in a pew halfway down the North aisle. Johnny noted with some amusement that Ann was being told off a lot. She wouldn't sit still. Her eyes darted all over the church, hunting dragons.

Glorious November sunshine awaited them at the end of Mass. Johnny and Ann escaped the confines of church, while Mr and Mrs Thornton queued up to shake hands with the priest.

"Oh no, Johnny, look at the bonty!" Ann squealed. Her outstretched finger pointed to the sodden skeleton of wooden ribs that made up S. Margaret's bonfire. Johnny had to agree. It really did look bad, even the railway sleeper was as black as mahogany and soaked slick.

"Maybe Mr. Middleton will use petrol to get it going. At least our firewood is sheltered."

Ann clapped her hands. "We can bring it here."

"No way! I'm not raiding from our own bonty."

"But what if the fire won't light, even with petrol, and the dragon gets out and eats all the virgins?"

Johnny was about to answer, when the ground lurched under his feet. The bell in the church tower clanged in startled fright, and a slate slithered down the Lady Chapel roof and smashed onto the gravestone below. Parishioners emerged from the main doors and south porch, scurrying like ants from a nest in the face of a boiling kettle.

"Johnny, it's the dragon. It's the dragon!" Ann wailed, one small voice of fear in an ocean of adult panic.

"It's an earthquake!" yelled one man.

"It's the pit!" contradicted another.

Sunday jackets were torn off and thrown to family members. The mine workers were all of one mind and set off at a run toward Collier Hill. Something had gone horribly wrong in the belly of the earth. Was anyone down there, even on a Sunday? Dour-faced parishioners scurried along the pavements, swarming toward the mine.

Mrs. Thornton scooped up Ann and Johnny in her wake. "Your dad will need his tool kit from the house. Johnny, you need to look after Ann while I take it to him and find out what's going on."

"But mummy," Ann tried to reason, "we've got to keep the dragon in its lair, or it might gobble up daddy and his friends."

Mrs. Thornton was in no mood for childish conversations, and wove between the slower pedestrians at a pace that the children had to jog to keep up with. She flew into the house and grabbed the tool box from the pantry, along with a little bread, some cheese, and beer. The bulky load bumped against her thighs as she struggled back onto the street. She ignored the coal-dust patches that her husband's toolbox smeared on her Sunday best. Johnny and Ann watched her determined waddle up the street toward the pit head.

Ann was crying. Her wet eyes bore into Johnny until he couldn't stand it any more. "Lets change our clothes and go and get our bonty wood."

Ann threw her skinny arms around him. "Oh, I knew you'd save us! You're just like St. George."

Johnny untangled himself and put on a serious expression. "If I'm a knight then you're my squire, and that means no whining, no whinging, and no saying 'No' when I ask you to do something. If you don't do what I say, you're not coming with me."

Ann was aghast. "I'll be good. I'll help you save everyone."

With the matter settled the two changed into their less-than-best clothes, and stole away to the sheltered stock of firewood that they had been hoarding for weeks. It was a good spot; none of the other gangs had found it. It was with some satisfaction and relief that they fond the whole lot bone dry after the storm.

Johnny had borrowed Granddad Bill's wheelbarrow from his allotment some days back. It proved useful when cobcoaling, not just for the bits of kindling they were given, but to pop Ann atop, dressed as the Guy. People commented on how life-like she was, and even Johnny had to admit that she had perfected the knack of a glassy stare and not breathing. Now the barrow was invaluable; they stocked it as high as it would go, and Johnny set off with a wobbly lurch. Ann's job was to pick up the bits of wood that kept sliding off and falling out.

In less than ten minutes they were in S. Margaret's churchyard. It was as if Parish Mass had happened days ago; the place was deserted. Ann's eyes scoured the place for signs of Mr. Middleton, but he wasn't around. They went over to the spot where the dead bonfire rotted. No amount of petrol would bring it back to life.

"We'll have to build a new one," Johnny announced, and started removing the larger pieces of wood that hindered the construction of the new fire. They crunched down what they could into ashes in the pit, and hurled the bits that wouldn't crumble into a new pile of cast-offs. It was hard work. Johnny wished he'd grabbed a bottle of pop for them both. The charcoal kissed him and Ann all over. The whites of their eyes and teeth were the only clean spots to be found on them.

"We look like the miners," Ann squealed with glee.

"Miners dig, we're building. Pass me the little bits of twigs to put in the middle. We'll make a nest of them and put the larger bits of wood on the outside like a wig-wam."

The ground shook again.

The wheelbarrow clanged and clattered. Ann cried, her tears running greasy tracks down her dirty cheeks. "Hurry, Johnny! It's coming. It's coming to get us!"

Johnny re-doubled his efforts, throwing stave after stave of wood onto the new fire's frame. Ann did as she was told. She passed him wood without complaint of it splintering her, or being too heavy. Between them, they had new fire ready in less than an hour.

The pair stood back to admire their work. Ann found the old piece of Spanish in her pocket and shared it. "Johnny, it's wonderful."

Their mouths smiled with gritty grins, but not for long. A stone dropped from nowhere between their feet. Then another hit Ann full in the belly. It took Johnny only a moment to comprehend what was going on. He pulled Ann to the ground, shielded his eyes and scanned the horizon for their assailants. Washbrook gang. Oh, no you don't, he thought, You're not getting your hands on this bonty.

Johnny could take on any of the Washbrook lot in a fair fight, but there was nothing fair about five against one, no matter how scrawny they were. It was the wiry ones you had to watch: those whose mothers and fathers didn't love them enough to feed them up. They were the ones who had a kind of wall-eyed madness, who wouldn't quit hitting, who wouldn't think to quit hitting.

Ann tugged at his arm as the children weighed each other up for the impending fight. "Tell me what to do, Sir knight."

"We're not playing knight and dragons, Ann. Do you know how to fight?"

"Jimmy Cardiff showed me. He said to keep my thumb outside of my fist—that way I won't break it when I hit someone on the nose."

Johnny smiled. "Good advice, but have you ever been in a fight?" Ann shook her head, and kept her eyes downcast.

Johnny continued, "You'll be fine. Just remember that there's no such thing as a 'dirty trick'. Boys will pull your hair, but you can kick them down there. If they come in close, like wrestlers, punch them in the kidneys, because that really hurts, and if you can get a couple of bites in, then do it - bite anything made of flesh. The most important thing is not to stop fighting. Don't stop fighting before they do."

Another stone landed between them on the ground where they lay. The salvo was accompanied with a declaration of war. "Oi! Bugger off and we won't hurt you."

"No one steals from S. Margaret's bonty. You know that. So why don't you clear off?"

A fresh hail of stones was hurled in response. "Their bonty went out. That bonty isn't theirs, so now it's ours."

As if of one mind, the Washbrook gang charged. They came through the railings, bobbing and weaving through the headstones toward Ann and Johnny. The pair got to their feet, ready to meet the enemy. Johnny was impressed to see that Ann had her left fist ready, thumb out, and had grabbed a chunk of wood with her right to make a cudgel. "Flippin' heck, Ann. Make sure they don't get hold of it and use it on you."

Johnny knew them by sight, not name, and had invented nick names for them. 'Terry' was like a rabid terrier: all bone and sinew held together with snot and a vicious streak of terror. He was going for Ann, but another boy got there first. He'd been christened 'Slim' on account of him being chubby and short. He probably fancied his chances fighting a little girl. Johnny watched his pudgy fists flay at her, but Ann's retaliatory ones landed with determination. She let fly, and the boy was soon scrambling back from her. Slim's crony, a young lad with buck teeth was new and hadn't earned a nickname yet. He taunted Ann, but seemed reluctant to let any of her punches connect with him. That left three on one for Johnny. These included, 'Mort', a lad with an ugly face that resembled the Blackpool footballer, Stanley Mortenson's, pet bull dog, 'Churchill', a boy with a fat round face and no hair, and, of course, Terry the terrier.

Terry shot at Johnny like an arrow. He caught him square in the midriff with his shoulder. The pair collapsed to the ground in a ball of kicking legs and wheeling arms. Johnny used his weight advantage to roll on top of Terry, but soon felt the stranglehold of Mort's arm around his neck. He punched out behind him, all the while trying to keep Terry pinned by his weight, but the half-Nelson grip was a good one and Mort soon yanked Johnny to his feet, freeing Terry. Nothing slowed Terry down, and so, as Johnny fought against Mort's grip, Terry pummelled his fists into Johnny's gut and face. Johnny could taste blood. He was sure a tooth was loose.

Mort let go and Johnny was free. Ann had seen off her attackers and was now beating the wrestler across his back with her home-made cudgel. Once more, Johnny and Terry resumed their grudge match. Both stayed on their feet, and although Terry was fast, Johnny was powerful. He timed it just right and delivered a kick to Terry's ribs that sent him sailing back against a gravestone, too winded to rise again.

A booming voice thundered over the battlefield, "Clear off you kids! I know your mothers. I'll be round to have a word with them."

It was Mr. Middleton. Ann and Johnny had never been so glad to see him. The Washbrook gang scrambled to their feet and ran out of the churchyard as fast as they could. Ann put her cudgel back on the newly built bonfire.

"You two, come here, now, before I get a grip of you!" They did as they were told, but remained out of reach of the massive man's span. He screwed his eyes up to look at them. "I know you two, but you look like a couple of gypsies."

Ann beamed at him through her mask of dirt. "It's me, Mr—Ann Thornton. You gave me a good whacking yesterday." She ran toward him and threw her arms around his waist. "And today you saved me from the bad boys."

Mr. Middleton picked her arms off him and put her to one side. "I'll not have to give you a good hiding today, will I? Looks like you've been playing in the fire again."

"Oh, we weren't playing," Johnny piped up. "We've brought the wood from our bonty, so we can save yours."

Ann tugged at the older man's sleeve to pull him toward the newly erected bonfire. "Now the dragon won't get out, and all those virgins won't get eaten like S. Margaret."

Mr. Middleton allowed himself to be taken to see the children's handiwork, and was openly impressed by their efforts. "It looks as if we'll have a bonfire after all. But you two best get home and washed before your mother sees you like that."

Ann shrugged. "She's at the pit with everybody else." "Not any more. Part of the mine collapsed, but no one was down there. They'll dig it out tomorrow." Johnny and Ann looked at each other with wide eyes, taking in the spectacle of their distressed wardrobe. They bolted.

"I'll make sure you two have the best spot at the bonty," Mr. Middleton called out after their retreating backs.

Two hours later, and smelling strongly of carbolic soap, the Thornton family joined their friends and neighbours back at S. Margaret's. The new fire blazed happily, and true to his word, Mr. Middleton saved a good spot for them to watch it from. Potatoes had been indiscriminately launched into hungry orange belly of the bonfire. Children cracked their teeth on sharp slabs of black treacle toffee, their greedy hands picking at crumbs from numerous trays of sliced parkin. The deacon wielded a red-hot poker, which he dipped with flair and a sizzle into the men's ale mugs to warm it. Johnny and Ann's skin prickled with heat, while their stomachs filled out happily.

Ann drew closer to her brother, her hot breath warming his ear. "Johnny, you really are a hero, you know. Just think about how awful it would be if we were all being eaten tonight, instead of doing the eating."

Johnny smiled down at her and ruffled her hair. "You're a hero, too. I think you're the best fighter amongst the girls. Next year, I bet Jimmy Cardiff will let you be a guard for the bonty wood."

Ann watched Mrs. Wakefield tie her blue scarf tighter over her head. It proved a difficult task, because she was holding the newest descendent of the booming Wakefield family, while her children's puppy bounded between her legs. Ann grinned a treacle grin. "At least all the virgins are safe."

Cob Coaling Song
We come a cob coaling for bonfire time,
Your coal and your money we hope you enjoy.
Fal a dee, fal a day, fal a diddle aye do day.
Down in yon' cellar there's an old umbrella
And down in yon' cellar there's an old pepper pot;
Pepper pot, pepper pot, morning 'till night
If ye give us nought we'll steal nought and bid you good-night!

Author's Note

1. As sung by S. Margaret's Silver Ladies (including those from Washbrook!)

2. I have not used the familiar shortened form of saint (St.), because I was brought up to use a single capital (S.) because the priest would go nuts at the idea of a saint looking like a street name.

Amanda Carr

THE LONG DARK NIGHTS

Agantia was preparing herself for her Dark Nights Ceremony. She felt a mixture of excitement tinged by more than a little fear. This was an event in a young girl's life when following the onset of menstruation, she would be directed by the elders of her tribe of the time and place. The Ceremony had acquired its name from the fact that it was always held at the time of the Dark Moon, when the waning moon finally disappeared into the night sky, plunging the land into darkness and then gradually the sliver of a new moon would appear to herald the moon's transition into its waxing phase. Following the three days and nights spent in contemplation, prayer and fasting the child would emerge as an adult with the chosen profession of, warrior, dreamer or bard of the tribe. The Warrior was the fighter/protector of the tribe, the Dreamer was the gate keeper of the tribe, the one that held sway between the living and the dead, and the one that talked to Spirits and read the signs in nature to predict the future. The Bards were the singers and storytellers who maintained the oral tradition of their people; they were the keepers of history. All her 14 years had been working towards this ceremony; everyone went through it, boys as well as girls although they of course merely had to wait for their 14th birthday and not for their menstruation to start!

It was well past harvest time and autumn had descended upon the land with her glorious colours of red, yellow, orange and gold, this would be the last ceremony of the year as winter time was considered too cold and dangerous for a child to spend three nights out in the forest alone. This year of course there was the added danger of the occupation by Rome and her soldiers, but apart from the small fort at Rigodunum, there had been little evidence of the great

Roman Army. The fort which had been originally wooden had been replaced by the current stone building and there were only about 80 soldiers billeted there with their centurion in charge. The Centurion had moved his household which contained not only his wife and children, but his servants and slaves too. Some of the local trades' people traded with the camp and of course the camp attracted its usual camp followers, the willing and the coerced.

The lands of the Brigante were wild and mountainous and had so far discouraged a full scale attack by a large force and the Brigantian Queen Cartimandua favoured compliance with Rome whilst her husband, Venutius of the Carvetti did not, both sides knew that more war was to come, it was just a question of time.

All the children, Agantia included had sat around the round house fire and listened to the stories of war, the bravery of their warriors, the depravity of the aggressors who were portrayed as evil personified in the songs the bards sang late into the night. Like the other children, Agantia had been carried asleep from the warmth of the fire to her bed, first in the nursery where the babies and young children slept watched over by nursing mothers, then later in the women's dormitory where as she approached adulthood she was allowed to progress. The boys followed a similar pattern and ended up in the men's dormitory a few months short of their 14th birthday. Life was very communal within the round house and ruled by a council consisting of the elders and the younger men and women of the community.

Agantia's father, Belboudiko was the smith who worked at the nearby forge, making horseshoes, brooches, torcs and hunting knives and since the war, arrow heads, spears and swords. His was an important trade,

103

and assured him of a position of respect upon the council. He was a tall, well built man with a shock of bright red hair and a matching beard. He had clear blue eyes that seemed to bore into your very soul and he made a very impressive figure when dressed for war with his sword, shield, spear and long, deadly sharp hunting and skinning knife which hung from his highly polished leather belt.

Agantia's mother, Voria was a dreamer of the Brigante and had spent several years on the Island of Mona being trained by the Druids. She had not taken Agantia with her but had left her first born daughter, in the care of Belboudiko's family. Agantia was born of a springtime romance between her parents that hadn't even survived the customary betrothal of a year and a day. The community made it a responsibility placed equally on both the boy's and the girl's family, so these children of short lived liaisons did not suffer. It did however, lead sometimes to a more fragmented family life, where the child was often moved between the families when new relationships were formed.

Belboudiko had gone through a hand fasting ceremony with a fiery female warrior called Beladora who he believed was his true love and soul mate. They enjoyed a lively, loving relationship that had produced two sons and a daughter and it was into this family that Agantia had been consigned when her mother left for Mona. She had been six years old and although she knew Belboudiko as her father she had lived with Voria, her mother and her mother's female lover, Avonicca and so it was a great shock to suddenly be thrust into the heart of a new family. She had been painfully shy of her half brothers, but her half sister was only a baby and she had made herself useful by caring for the child. Beladora had found her new step daughter a strange little creature, marked out already by the elders as a dreamer. She was a quiet, reflective child not used to the rough and tumble of a mixed household. She had moved from the safety of the round house and the female dormitory into the living quarters at the rear of the forge and life had been strange and a little frightening at first. Her father when she got to know him, was not such a terror as she had first thought, he enjoyed the company of his little daughter and found her a good help mate. She was obedient and eager to please him and she progressed from tne very menial tasks of the forge, to making simple brooches and small blades. She had an eye for pattern and colour and she understood about finding the song within the metal and working with it to produce beautiful results.

Beladora when not involved in fighting or bringing up her children, spent her time gathering herbs and plants and making potions and compresses to heal and restore people to good health. Agantia was fascinated by how the plants and herbs worked and proved an eager and willing student and so grew a bond between the girl child and her step mother. Agantia was happy, she had found a place in her father's family and was loved not only by him, but by his wife and other children and so her life progressed for the next seven years until she was thirteen and then her happy world came crashing down around her ears. Her mother returned from Mona.

Voria had sent word to Agantia whenever someone was leaving Mona for the mainland, but these messages had been few and far between. Voria returned with Avonicca. Both women had passed through their training as dreamers of Mona and now slipped back into the life in the round house and Voria expected her daughter to join her. For the first time in her life Agantia had rebelled and refused to go. Although her father and Beladora didn't want her to go either they felt that Voria had a right to expect her daughter to return to live with her. Upset beyond tears she had turned to the Grandmother, Riganmelta who was her maternal grandmother and a member of the community council and begged her for help. The Grandmother had said that it was a matter that the council could resolve but that by asking for their help, Agantia must abide by their decision. The distressed girl readily agreed.

The day of the council dawned and all parties went to the meeting to put forward their side of the story. Agantia made an impassioned plea to be allowed to remain with her father and Beladora at the forge. She explained how much she loved her brothers and little sister and how she had learned not only smith craft but also how to be a healer's assistant and that by staying there she could continue to improve. Both Belboudiko and Beladora supported her request. When it was Voria's turn, she said that she had looked after the child the first six years of her life and now having completed her dreamer's training she was well placed to help develop her daughter's dreaming which she claimed Belboudiko had woefully neglected. The council retired to make a decision. After an hour, the council was reconvened and all parties stood in front of them to hear the pronouncement.

The Grandmother told Agantia that she must spend six months of the year with her mother during which she could learn her dreaming role, then six months with her father when she could continue with her other studies. Each week during the six months she could spend 2 days with the other parent which, according to the Grandmother, would keep the ties alive with both parents. Agantia accepted the decision although she was sad that the first six months would be spent with her mother and she longed for the two days she could return to her father and Beladora.

The twelve months passed quickly enough and the bond between mother and daughter was reintroduced and grew. With the help of Riganmelta her Grandmother and Voria, her mother Agantia learned the craft of the dreamer. She learned the art of meditation and visualisation and how to connect with spirits, how to read signs in nature and had to agree with both her mother and grandmother that she did have the gift for it. As her bond with her mother strengthened, her bond with her father and stepmother remained steadfast. The only fly in the ointment was her relationship with Avonicca. She did not like the woman and had to admit she was jealous of the love and attention that her mother lavished upon her. Avonicca tried hard to get on with Agantia but she had no children of her own and had never wanted any and she found herself jealous of her lover's growing relationship with her daughter. Although she had never said it, mainly because at the time her opinion had not been sought, she would have preferred that Agantia had remained with her father and just visited a couple of times a month but she kept this to herself and bided her time, she hoped the girl could be pushed into a relationship following her admission into adulthood and once pregnant would be someone else's problem. Avonicca decided to make this object her number one priority, with Agantia's Dark Nights approaching. Then, with the daughter out of the way she and Voria could go back to the blissful life they had enjoyed on Mona.

Agantia gazed at the long, silver coloured blade with its honed and sharpened double edges. This was her very own hunting and skinning knife that she had made herself for the approaching ceremony. She placed it on the bearskin spread on the ground at the mouth of the forge. She wiped the sweat from her forehead with the back of her hand. The forge, even in the depths of winter could be too warm and make one sweat. She gazed down at her growing cache of possessions. Lying on the bearskin alongside the knife was a small, superbly crafted short bladed sword which Belboudiko had lovingly produced for his eldest daughter. It was specifically designed for her height and weight. Despite being a practical man, the Smith had allowed his artistic nature to take hold and had carved a beautiful, intricate pattern that contained elements of her dreaming, the owl, the raven and the swirling currents of the river on the hilt and blade of the weapon. It was a masterpiece, quite the most intricate and beautiful thing he had ever made and he was very proud of it.

Next to the sword, lay a matching trio of torcs, one for her neck and two for her upper arms. Made of solid silver because of her name, they were carved with signs of her dreaming in copper and studded with green semi precious stones. They were a joint project by father and daughter and had been designed with love. The neck torc had been made by the father and the arm torcs by the daughter. They were exquisite, the dark glowing green stones a reflection of the colour of Agantia's eyes. Next to these lay her new wool tunic, it was black and edged with green, as near a match to the green on the torcs as could be made. She had tried it on previously and had seen her reflection in the river water; it suited her pale luminous white skin and her bright red hair and those lovely green eyes. One of her brothers had shined up her leather belt and the ornate scabbards that held her blades had been shined up too. The sword gleamed in the thin autumn sun and Agantia shivered a little as she rolled them all up in the bearskin and secured it with a leather strap. She took them round the back to the living quarters and placed them carefully upon her bed and then began to make preparations for their evening meal. Both her father and Beladora would be back soon with the children and she wanted the meal to be ready for their return.

As she prepared vegetables and herbs to go into the pot with the hare, her brothers had caught the other day, she was thoughtful. After her Dark Nights she would be approaching the end of her six month stay with her father and the beginning of the next stint with her mother. It troubled her this splitting of her life, but she could not help how she felt and the truth was she much preferred living with her father to with her mother and, although she loved her mother, she found the constant presence of her mother's lover caused her the jealous feelings she did not like to admit to. She had spoken to the Grandmother about how she felt and the elder woman had told her that she must learn to keep these feelings in check and not let it spoil her relationship with her mother.

"We do not always choose who we love," claimed the Grandmother, "one day you may experience this for yourself."

"But why could she not love my father and live with him as Beladora does?" Aguantia had appealed.

"Because that is the way people are sometimes child, your mother prefers the company and love of other women to that of men, some women love both men and women and have many lovers of both sexes, and some do not. This is the purpose of the betrothals to find out about your sexuality, you will find out your true nature that way too."

"Oh Grandmother, I haven't even thought about things like that for me!"

The Grandmother smiled her wise, elder smile, "Well, time enough after your Dark Nights child."

Agantia was so engrossed in her own thoughts that it was a moment or two before the sound of the hoof beats of a lone rider intruded upon them. Leaving the stew simmering away, she went to the entrance of the forge just in time to see the rider pull up his horse and dismount in one fluid movement. He had not seen her in the shadows of the entrance and for a moment she had the advantage and drew back into the shadows to view him better.

From his clothing and weaponry she knew he was not of her tribe, his sword and knife of a different style to theirs were she guessed of the Trinovantes, a tribe from the south. He was tall and with dark hair braided in the style of a warrior with the tell tale kill feathers woven into the braids. He was muscular and she thought his profile very handsome. She judged him to be a young warrior of 18 years old or so.

The young Celt scanned the outside of the forge and as he turned in a circle the other side of his face came into view. Agantia had to stifle the gasp that escaped her involuntarily. His handsome features on the right side of his face had been slashed by a knife or sword blade that had left a nasty scar that ran from his hairline, the length of his face to his chin. She realised he had heard her but still she hesitated to show herself.

"Smith! Smith! I give you greetings and come in peace, you have nothing to fear from me!" his voice had the melodic accent of more southern climes.

Agantia took a deep breath and still clutching her vegetable knife from her cooking, in her hand she appeared in the doorway of the forge and watched him spin round to face her, ever wary, his hand on the hilt of his sword, ready for action should the occasion demand. His dark brown eyes flecked with amber met her green cat like eyes and they weighed each other up warily. Despite the vegetable knife the Trinovantian decided that this Smith or Smith's apprentice was of no threat to him and he relaxed and smiled broadly. He released the hilt of his sword and making a fist with his right hand, placed it upon his chest where his heart was in the universal warrior's salute. Unsure of the etiquette of such a meeting and wondering if he was making fun of her, she nevertheless, put the knife in her left hand, made a fist with her right hand and returned the salute perfectly, maintaining eye contact with the Trinovantian and addressed him in a surprisingly strong voice.

"If indeed you come in peace then I, Agantia, daughter of the Smith and Warrior Belboudiko of the Brigantes, bid you welcome Warrior of the Trinovantes."

He was impressed by her intelligence and knowledge, she had recognised his warrior status from the braids and kill feathers, but many would have mistaken his accent. The lovely green eyes did not flinch and met his with a cat-like stare. She was quite small in stature, and he guessed she was about 14 or 15 years old. She had the white luminous skin of her race and beautiful fiery red hair that she wore in a thick braid that reached her waist. As the silence lengthened he realised he was being impolite and cleared his throat, the better to reply to her greeting.

"Thank you Agantia of the Brigante, I am indeed a Warrior of the Trinovantes, I am Belisarno."

"And what is it you need of a Smith?" asked Agantia

"My horse has lost a shoe, I need it replacing,"

"Well, I could do that for you, but you will have to wait for the fire to heat up, even if I use the bellows, it will take a while."

"I can wait."

And with that the bargain was struck. Agantia indicated a bench seat in the forge for him to wait upon and went to check on her stew before returning to the fire and heaping more charcoal on the still glowing embers. She took down the bellows and set to extracting a fierce heat from the glow. As soon as she deemed the fire hot enough she donned the leather apron that Beladora had made for her to wear in the forge and set about making a new horseshoe. Belisarno watched as the girl went about her work. She seemed to him to know what she was doing. She used economic movements and soon had the forge fire hot enough to shape the metal into a horseshoe after very competently checking the size of his horse's hooves by approaching the tethered horse to his flank and patting his neck and blowing gently into his nostrils before running a practised hand down his fetlock and raising his hoof off the ground to check the shoe size with her wooden measuring stick. Satisfied, she replaced the horse's hoof and crooned unintelligibly to the beast before returning to the forge to strike the shoe.

Belisarno watched as Agantia wielded a hammer that had been specially scaled down for her by her father and shaped a perfect horseshoe. When satisfied with the result, she plunged it into the waiting bucket of water and a huge spray of steam was released. Indicating that she would return when the shoe was cool enough she returned to her cooking pot, to give it a good stir. Raising the lid she was met with a steam of aromatic herbs, vegetables and the pieces of hare that she sniffed appreciatively. Giving the stew a good stir; she replaced the lid and returned to the forge. Belisarno was seated where she had left him, leaning against the wall of the forge, feeling warm and more than a little drowsy, he had been riding for at least three days and he was tired and hungry. The smell of the cooking stew had not escaped his nostrils and he felt his stomach rumbling emptily.

When Agantia had the shoe ready she requested that he come and help her steady the horse. He needed no second bidding and sprang to his feet to assist. And this is how her family came upon them. The boys riding their ponies at the front and their little sister on the back of her mother's horse whilst their father brought up the rear on the huge stallion he always rode. Agantia had just finished shoeing the horse and had straightened up at the sound of her family's return. She waved and smiled and both warriors relaxed, their immediate thoughts of danger dissipating at her manner of greeting.

The noise of the boys spooked the horse and he tried to break free of his tether, but Belisarno hung on tight and Agantia stroked the horse's nose making those soothing noises she had made before to calm the beast. Once the adults had dismounted, Agantia effected the introductions and winced for the young warrior as both Belboudiko and Beladora couldn't help but be affected by the difference between one side of his face to the other. It showed in the slight recoil in their faces. Agantia hoped her dismay had not been as obvious as she had the shadows of the forge to hide her first reaction. The Smith checked his young daughter's work and Belisarno saw how anxious she was for her father's approval which Belboudiko gave wholeheartedly. Meanwhile the boys had tended to the horses and fed them whilst Beladora exclaimed with pleasure at the cooking stew which was all but ready to serve.

The Smith and Trinovantian Warrior negotiated a price for the work and the Smith accepted a lovely pewter and copper brooch in payment and vowed to give it to his daughter afterwards, for a job well done. Belboudiko asked Belisarno to stay for dinner and the young warrior accepted gratefully. They ate their meal and Belboudiko quizzed his young guest about what had brought him into the land of the Brigantes, He explained that his mother and sister had both died of the winter fever last year and that now he had no reason to stay at home under the heel of Roman occupation.. He explained that both he and his father had fought against the Romans in the earlier battles in the land of the Trinovantes, and that his father had died as the result of wounds inflicted.

"There will be war again and this time everyone will be involved, north and south, and I am here to offer my services to the Brigantes. Do you think they will accept me?" Belisarno suddenly looked like the young man he was and Belboudiko clapped him on the shoulder smiling.

"I am sure they will, in fact I will speak for you at the council and recommend that they do just that, Anyone can see you have earned the title of warrior. Did you have no dreamer to bring with you?"

"My sister was my dreamer and so no, I am a warrior without a dreamer."

Agantia blushed furiously as she saw the adults exchange a look and then smile conspiratorially. They were the limit, they really were. She just hoped Belisarno had not noticed. After they had eaten, Belboudiko took the young man to the round house to introduce him to the community and find him a bed for the night. The Smith didn't return until much later, his face flushed from the fire and the beer he had drunk. Agantia had gone to bed, but she carefully strained to hear his conversation with Beladora and discovered that the young warrior had been welcomed and had been given a bed for the night and that her father would be speaking with the council about him after the ceremony of the Dark Nights which was now only a day away.

Next day dawned fine but cold and Agantia hoped the rain would stay away for the next three days and nights she was to spend in the woods alone. She breakfasted and then went to see her mother who had requested her presence. The talk of the round house among both men and women was about the arrival of the Trinovantian, and Agantia as the Smith's daughter was welcomed as a source of further knowledge, but they were disappointed as she knew no more than they did. Some opposed his request to join the Brigantes when the inevitable war came, some did not want to even think of war and some mistrusted his motives. One of these was Avonicca, herself an outsider, she had come from the Carvetti in the north, and although the Carvetti had originally been of the Brigante tribe now they had their own lands they were considered as separate. Avonicca thought he could be a Roman spy and intended to say so at the council. Agantia was furious and although normally respectful of her elders she was stung to tell her that she was wrong. Both Voria and Avonicca were surprised at the vehemence of her defence of the Trinovante and when Avonicca said sarcastically,
"Any one would think you had a fancy for Scarface!"

Agantia raged back, "His name is Belisarno, not Scarface and I haven't got a fancy for him, I just think he tells the truth, you can see it in his eyes!"

Avonicca rolled her eyes skywards and replied, "Oh you can see it in his eyes can you?"

Voria, seeing her daughter's distress, stopped her lover with a reproachful look and took the girl to one side to talk her through the details of the forthcoming ceremony and what would happen afterwards.

When she was returning to the forge in the late afternoon, she came across Belisarno in the company of about 12 or more youths, some older than him but most younger, hanging on to his every word as they begged for more stories of war. Most of them had so far avoided war but they would all have to fight in the future, in the war to end all wars which were coming. Agantia smiled in his direction and he raised his arm in salute and bid her good afternoon. With all eyes upon her she tried hard not to blush, but it was no good; the more she tried not to the redder she got until her skin matched the red of her hair. She hurried on embarrassed, as the boys called after her, giggling at her discomfiture. The boys escorted Belisarno back to the round house, where he was feted by several families and again invited to tell war stories by the fire. Later on he begged to be excused and went to his bed space. He sat for a while contemplating his next course of action. He had found out that tomorrow Agantia took part in her Dark Nights Ceremony and went to spend three days and nights in the woods. The little he knew of her, he liked and he wanted to present her with a gift but was not sure how it would be received and the last thing he wanted to do was offend her or her family of warriors.

He pondered for a little while longer and then getting to

his feet, he sheathed his hunting knife in his belt and huddled into his warm cloak and walked the short distance from the round house to the forge, keeping to the shadows so he wouldn't be seen. Just as he was wondering how best to do what he had come to do, he detected a movement at the rear of the forge and heard the low menacing growl of one of the hounds that Belboudiko allowed to roam free at night. He froze, the hounds were war hounds, bred to fight and protect, and he didn't fancy being perceived as an enemy. Although there was no moon that night his eyes had grown accustomed to the night and he caught sight of Agantia; he could make out the silhouette of her form and that of the hound, she appeared other worldly and he drew in his breath sharply. He called her name quietly. She heard him right away as did the hound by her side. With her hand on his neck, she hissed for him to be quiet and for the benefit of Belisarno she said aloud,

"This is no enemy Dago, it is our friend the Trinovantian Warrior taking the air." there was warmth and laughter in her voice.

He smiled into the darkness, "I am glad to be perceived a friend by the brave hound of the Brigante, but you do well to protect your mistress."

He emerged from the shadows so she could see him and the hound convinced by his mistress he was a friend, sniffed his hand and wagged his long tail. Belisarno, who loved animals stroked the dog's head and scratched his ears.

"What brings you to the forge this evening?" asked Agantia coquettishly, "More horseshoes?"

He smiled again, "No not tonight, I come on a different

quest." Agantia merely raised her eyebrows in silent question.

He found himself suddenly shy, "Yes, I am told it is the ceremony of your Dark Nights tomorrow and that you go into the forest for three days and nights on your own?"

"Yes, that's right. Do your tribes do something similar?"

"Yes, we do." he paused suddenly unsure of how to go on, "You mustn't be afraid, it seems like a long time but it will soon pass and then you will emerge a dreamer and adult member of the tribe. It is a great honour to go through."

"Oh I am not afraid!"

"Well, no sorry, maybe that was the wrong choice of word, but you must have caution, alone in the woods."

She laughed, "You sound like my mother! She has been filling my head with dire warnings and instructions about my dreaming. Did you always know you were destined to be a warrior?"

"Always. And you, a dreamer?"

"It appears I was born to it, according to my mother."

"And which warrior will you become dreamer to?"

"I do not know, although Avonicca has some Carvetti warrior in mind. The warriors if there is more than one who wish me to become their dreamer must present their case to council and it will be decided there."

"Do you not have a say in the matter?"

"Oh yes, as an adult, I will be able to speak for the first time in council and may express my preference, if there is more than one warrior seeking me as his dreamer."

Agantia held her breath, had she said enough? Did he understand what she wanted of him? She wasn't sure.

"There will be." Belisarno replied and Agantia let out her breath thankfully.

He produced a small package and offered it to her. Wordlessly she took it and unwrapped it carefully. The silver owl brooch gleamed. It was beautifully crafted and had all the intricate markings of a very life like owl."

"It was my sister's," his voice husky with emotion, "she was my dreamer before she died of the fever, she too had the owl in her dreaming as you do. It has been cleansed." He added anxious that she would find nothing wrong with his gift.

Agantia found her voice, "It's beautiful, really lovely, so intricately made, but if I accept it that would bind me to accept you as my warrior?"

Belisarno shook his head, "Nothing binds you Agantia unless you wish it so. I offer this as a mark of friendship and respect between us and I shall make my request to the council along with the Warrior of the Carvetti and whoever else claims the honour."

"Thank you," Agantia whispered closing her hand over the brooch, "I would like that very much."

The hound at her side quivered as he heard the Smith coming out of the forge.

"Who have we here?" boomed the Smith making both of them jump, "You don't have suitors already daughter and you not through your Dark Nights yet, do you?"

Agantia being used to her father's teasing smiled in exasperation into the dark. Meanwhile Belisarno emerged from the darkness so the Smith could see him properly.

"It is I, Belisarno of the Trinovantes, and I would do nothing to offend you Belboudiko Smith and Warrior of the Brigantes."

The Smith clapped the younger man on the back in a friendly gesture. "You mustn't mind me Belisarno; I am just an anxious father looking after his daughter's interests."

"Of course."

The Smith offered to accompany the young Warrior on his walk back to the round house, and Belisarno with his mission completed agreed. Bidding Agantia goodnight, the two men left her to return to the fire and the company of her stepmother.

The next morning dawned bright and cold and Agantia, who had spent a disturbed night tossing and turning, was quick to rise and wash and dress, eager for the ceremony to start. Following a hearty breakfast she checked her bearskin roll and wrapped her cloak around her and fixed it in the fashion of the Brigante with the owl brooch placed high upon the left shoulder. She prepared her horse, a strong Welsh cob, and went in search of her parents. She found both her mother and father in heated discussion while Beladora and

Avonicca stood back allowing the two to speak undisturbed.

Agantia stood apart from the little group and scanned the area around the round house. Various people bid her good morning. Avonicca, who rarely missed anything, noticed the lovely silver brooch on her shoulder and enquired where it had come from. Unable to be rude to the woman Agantia replied quietly that it had been a gift and, when pressed, admitted it was from the Trinovante.

"So Scarface wants you for his dreamer?" Avonnica demanded sharply, "He is presumptuous, giving a gift before the ceremony and without your parents' approval."

"He has my father's approval, " Agantia retorted.

"I see, well Luko of the Carvetti has your mother's!" Avonicca beckoned the youth forward and Luko walked forward to stand in front of Agantia. Unlike the Trinovante he made no warrior's salute, merely inclined his head and offered her a wrapped gift.

Agantia took the package and thanked the youth. At Avonicca's insistence she opened the gift to reveal the leather thong of the dreamer made from plaited leather with semi precious stones of blue and brown hanging from it. Taken aback Agantia stammered her thanks. Avonicca insisted that she wear it and wouldn't take no for an answer telling her that she must treat both warriors the same and if she wore Scarface's brooch she must also wear Luko's dreamer's thong. Unable to argue with such logic, Agantia pulled the thong over her head.

Thankfully, Agantia noticed that her parents had finished

their discussion and were walking towards them. They were being urged to hurry up as it was time for the ceremony to begin and so without further ado, they walked to the round house entrance where the elders of the tribe were awaiting them. It fell to the oldest of the elders to make the speech and that happened to be Riganmelta, Agantia's Grandmother. Riganmelta called everyone to order, her authoritative voice silencing the crowd that had gathered.

"Who brings the child to her Dark Nights?" Riganmelta asked as a start to the ceremony.

Voria stepped forward, "I, Voria, of the Brigantes, also Dreamer of Mona and mother to this child bring her,"

"Child of Voria step forward!"

Agantia stepped forward.

"Are you, Agantia, daughter of Belboudiko the Warrior and Voria the Dreamer of Mona both of the Brigante tribe, ready to sit your Dark Nights?"

"I am."

"Do you understand that when we leave you at the entrance to the forest you must spend the next three days and three nights on your own, without the help or assistance of any living being?"
"I do"

"Are you already called?"

"I am, I am already called to be a dreamer."

"Will you accept the council's interpretation of what befalls you during your Dark Nights even if this may contradict that calling?"

"I will."

"Then Agantia, eldest girl child of Belboudiko and Voria go to your Dark Nights with the blessing of this council of whom I am representative, go in the protection of the Great Mother Goddess of the Earth and the Great Father God of the Sky, and return safely as dreamer, warrior, or bard, of the great tribe of the Brigante which is your birthright."

Agantia inclined her head and then led by her mother on one side and her stepmother on the other they walked to where the horses waited. Once mounted the horses walked in procession, followed on foot by all the girls and women of the tribe. They began to sing a song that was sung for every girl on the way to her Dark Nights. The noise of singing reverberated around the countryside and could not help but lift the soul of any who heard it. It was a song of hope, of love, of coming to the end of childhood and standing on the brink of womanhood, of making promises to the Gods and dedicating one's life to one's calling whatever that might be. The men and the boys of the tribe followed at a respectable distance. The reverse occurred when it was a boy's Dark Nights. At last the forest came into view and, as they drew close the procession pulled up and allowed the song to reach its conclusion. Agantia dismounted and gathered up her bearskin roll and slung it over her shoulder, it still contained the torcs and her sword, her knife was hanging from her belt beneath the folds of her cloak, so she would have immediate protection should she need it. The torcs would be worn upon her return in celebration of the completion of the Dark

Nights. The men and boys surged forward and became intermingled with the women and girls and they all waved and shouted encouraging instructions as with a final wave, Agantia entered the forest and disappeared from view.

Both Agantia's parents suffered during the next three days and nights wondering how their daughter fared in the forest, despite all the good advice they had both offered her. Belboudiko's advice had been of a more practical nature, like going deep into the forest where she might find a cave to shelter in, that would protect her from the elements and attentions of any wild animals or of anyone else for that matter. Voria had been more concerned with her daughter's psychological well being, and she had instructed her to use her time wisely, in the pursuit of her dreaming.

Agantia like all the Brigante children had been instructed in self preservation from a young age. She was an accurate shot with a stone and sling, could skin an animal with her knife, so she was not expected to starve. She had also been taught how to use the weapons she carried to defend herself if need be and although, not called to be a warrior, she had received her basic warrior training like the rest. In times of war the children would come to the battlefield and it was considered preferable to either kill the children, or let them be killed in battle, rather than let them fall into the hands of the enemy who might rape and enslave them.

It was the morning of the third day with only one more night to go that Voria had wakened from a terrible nightmare that left her visibly shaking. She begged Avonicca to fetch Belboudiko and, somewhat annoyed that her lover was seeking him for help rather than herself, she went reluctantly. When hearing of Voria's distress he came immediately and begged her to tell him what was wrong.

"I think she is dead!" Voria cried out.

"Agantia? No, no you are mistaken," Belboudiko replied patting her shoulder, in an attempt to comfort her; Avonicca glared but was totally ignored by both the distressed parents. "I saw her, in my dream, she was dead I tell you and I can't reach her no matter what I do!"

"Did you see the Crow Goddess?" Asked Avonnica, anxiously.

Voria began to weep, "Yes, I saw the Bodua"

Belboudiko wanted to set out immediately to search for his daughter. However, even he knew that Voria wouldn't be the first hysterical mother who claimed her daughter was dead. In the past, parents had rushed off only to find their child safe and well; furious that her Dark Nights had been disturbed. Once disturbed, they had to be done again and with winter almost upon them it would be well into next year before Agantia would be able to do them again. He told both the women to use all of their dreaming powers to try and locate his daughter but warned that no-one was to go and seek her out. The elders of the council agreed with him. The Grandmother had said if the child had summoned Bodua it would be because her life was in danger; she would already be dead and there was nothing they could do about it. If there was some other explanation, then she would appear tomorrow morning from the forest safe and well.

Belboudiko sought out the Trinovante and. as he was not of the Brigantes the Smith thought if asked for Belisarno's help, he might be persuaded to go and look for his daughter. Belisarno agreed to go into the forest and try and find Agantia without her seeing him and if she was all right, then he

125

could return and if she was not, then the Smith gave him his permission to show himself in order to help her. With a promise of complete secrecy, Belisarno absented himself from the round house and the Brigantian settlement and on foot entered the forest by a circuitous route taking care not to be seen as he did so. Belisarno was a good hunter and tracker and after smearing his face with mud from the undergrowth he did his best to merge into the forest. He tracked through the forest hoping that he would find the girl safe and well and momentarily wondering why it suddenly mattered so much to him. He worked his way to where the line of trees met the mountains. Belboudiko had thought she would have sought refuge in one of the caves.

He moved noiselessly through the undergrowth taking care to blend in, he carried his knife in his right hand and felt the scar on his face ache as it always did before he went into battle. Something was very wrong, he could feel it. He paused, listening to the sounds of the forest and let his own heartbeats quieten as he strained to hear anything unusual. He heard a noise, a human noise; it sounded like a sob that was being stifled. It was coming from somewhere up ahead.. He moved forward slowly and carefully until he came to rest behind a large oak tree. He heard the sound again and looked up towards the mountain. As he strained his eyes to see, he caught sight of a faint wisp of blue smoke, a way up the mountain in what looked like a small opening. He advanced slowly, reluctant to leave the cover of the trees, knife held at the ready he progressed slowly and stealthily upwards. As he advanced he could see the small opening was actually the mouth of a cave partly obscured by a large boulder. As he drew nearer he realised that it hid the fire which was the source of the wisp of smoke. He approached the boulder like a fox, moving silently, until he saw the mouth of the cave behind it. The smoke was still merely a wisp from a fire of wood with peat on the top of it so that there would not be too much smoke to draw attention to it. The mouth of the cave wasn't very large and it seemed at first very dark. He paused to allow his eyes to adjust to the dim interior and listened intently again for the sound he had heard. The moments passed silently and just as he was beginning to think he had imagined the sob, he heard it again. He strained to see where in the cave it was coming from, when a sudden movement drew his eye as Agantia appeared at the cave entrance, her hand dashing tears from her eyes. He drew back so as not to be seen.

What should he do? Why was she crying? Was she just a bit lonely or frightened out here on her own? Had she hurt herself? Remembering his mission, he decided to watch her a while to see if he could determine what was actually wrong. At least she was alive! As she wiped away her tears and drew in a great big shuddering breath, he saw her face was dirty, there was a cut on her forehead that had been bleeding. Her hair always neatly braided was hanging down and looked wild and unruly. With every fibre of his being he wanted to put his arms around this girl-woman and comfort her. He wanted to keep her safe and he was surprised by the strength of his feelings, for which he had never previously had for anyone else, yet something kept him still.

He watched with horror as she suddenly raised both her hands in which he realised she held her own hunting knife, with the blade turned inwards. Her hands were shaking but it was obvious to Belisarno what she was about to do. Placing his own knife silently on the ground beside him he launched himself like an attacking wolf at the girl and brought both of them flat to the stony ground, thankfully hearing the clink of metal on the ground as his actions had dislodged the knife from her grip. He had knocked all the breath out of her but expected her next action when she recovered would be to scream, he placed his hand over her mouth. She lay unmoving with her eyes closed.

"Agantia, it's me," he whispered, "It's me, Belisarno!"

At the sound of his name her eyes flew open and once more his amber flecked brown eyes looked deep into her beautiful green ones, she burst into floods of tears and as he rolled off her and helped her into a sitting position so he could cradle her in his arms and stroke her hair and murmur comforting words softly into her ear, her body was shaking uncontrollably and her sobs were now coming loud and unrestrained. Belisarno knew he must wait for this emotional storm to abate before he would be able to get any sense out of her.

When her sobs had finally quietened, he listened incredulously to the story she told him. She had caught and killed a hare with her stones and sling on her first day and had hung the animal in the cave, to save for her meal on the third day. She had fasted for two days and two nights only drinking water or herbal tea. She made either nettle tea to detoxify her body or mugwort tea to concentrate her mind for her dreaming. Every thing had been going well. By the close of the second day she was feeling light headed from the lack of food; so she rested or, passed the time picking herbs and plants to make up her healing supplies. The previous night she had dreamed very well, she could not tell him of what, because he was not a dreamer and, she must discuss it with the dreamers. He should not have intruded on her Dark Nights although she assured him she was glad he had.

She had risen early this morning, and had taken a walk to clear her head, she had gone down to the river and washed her hands and face with the bitingly cold river water which had wakened her up. It was then she had heard the men in the forest. She judged there to be two on foot and her first instinct was to run away, but she realised she must not do any such thing as it would only give her away. She had left the river bank, slowly and carefully and had tried to melt into the undergrowth, placing each foot carefully so as not to be heard. The two men were not careful at all, they were uncaring if they were seen or not, which had made Agantia even more frightened. She had reached the foot of the cliff where the cave was above her and hesitated. She did not want them to discover her cave but it easily gave her the best cover.

She had taken a deep breath and then moving quickly had climbed swiftly up the rocky path. She had all but made it when her foot dislodged a stone, that in turn dislodged a few more and the noise had alerted the two men to her presence. She had made it to the cave and was able to grab her sword in one hand to join her knife which she already held at the ready in the other one. She had kept back from the cave entrance and had prayed to the Goddess to keep her safe and not let her be seen.

The men had climbed upwards toward the cave and she had seen with dismay they were two Roman soldiers. The shadows had hidden her for a few moments but then one of them had spied her and demanded she show herself. Trembling she had done just that. The men had been a little taken aback by the weaponry but had recovered when they had realised she was only a young girl and alone. She had been easily overcome by the soldiers.

Alarmed that they may still be near by, Belisarno asked, "Where are they now?"

In reply, she silently got to her feet, took his hand and led him into the depths of the cave. When his eyes had adjusted to the darkness, he could make out two bodies lying side by side.

"Dead?" his voice was incredulous, how could she have killed two Roman soldiers on her own?

"Dead." She replied quietly stifling another sob.

He drew her outside the cave again; the two of them sat by the fire whilst she finished her story. She found it hard to describe what the men had done to her, but Belisarno being acquainted with Roman soldiers, assured her he understood she had been violated by both men. She started to cry again, and he allowed her to do so for a while before pressing her to finish the tale. Damn these soldiers he thought why they had to rape a child when there were bound to be concubines back at their camp. She said that they had seen the hare and decided they were hungry. They had skinned it and cut it into pieces and then dragging her to her feet from the back of the cave where they had left her praying for death, they had demanded she cook them a meal. She had reached for her bag of herbs and at first they had been suspicious but when she had shown them the rosemary and other aromatic herbs they agreed she could use them.

"They did not know much about plants and herbs or they would have recognised the belladonna that I put in. I know it is poisonous and must be used in tiny amounts to make tinctures for the eyes for example, I had no idea if I could kill them with the amount I had, the herb is bitter but I put lots of root vegetables in the stew together with a lot of rosemary and they ate it, all of it, they seemed very hungry.

"They did not make you try it first?" asked Belisarno surprised at their stupidity. They must have been young and inexperienced he thought.

"No, they said I didn't need to eat where I was going. I believe they intended to kill me, that is why I summoned Bodua our War Goddess, the bringer of death, with her crows so that she could take my soul when I died. I wanted her to lead me home to the Summerlands." She replied.

"First one of them got to his feet clutching his throat and belly and screaming, the other realising what had happened to them lunged at me with his sword, but he missed and it fell from his hands. He fell to his knees and I grabbed the sword and plunged it into his chest as I was taught in my warrior training. I killed him. The other one lay on the ground and just to make sure he was dead, I took my hunting knife and slit his throat. I allowed their souls to leave their bodies by their wounds and asked the Bodua who once called must be appeased by a death to take them. She did and left me living.

"Then why were you about to kill yourself when I arrived?" Belisarno's voice was gentle and deeply concerned

"Because of the violation." she whispered.

"But it was not your fault, surely they will see that when we tell them?"

"No! No! We must tell them nothing of this, nothing, do you hear?"

"Well, if that is what you want Agantia but I don't understand."

131

"A girl must remain a virgin until she has passed through her Dark Nights. The punishment for not keeping yourself pure for your first betrothal is banishment from the tribe. The man concerned can be challenged and killed by my father, or other male member of my family. Or he could be branded and banished." Agantia's voice trembled, "A child, any child would be taken from me and brought up by the man's family or they would have to pay my family to bring it up. I would have brought dishonour to my family. The fact of them being Romans only complicates matters further"

Belisarno considered this information carefully. He knew that the Brigantes were strict about adhering to their laws and customs as was his own tribe but he also knew certainly within his own tribe how clemency would often be applied. Young men and women were permitted any number of betrothals before a final hand fasting and the children of such liaisons were always taken care of one way or another. Sometimes they were even being farmed out to childless couples who brought them up as their own. It was not uncommon for both young men and women to experience relationships with both sexes until they had decided upon their sexuality. The tribes were very clannish, but they loved children and the mortality rate was quite high. Every child was considered precious and given a chance to live. They tended to stick together in times of adversity even while laying the law down with a heavy hand to discourage those young people that broke it.

Deciding that first of all they needed to be practical and get rid of the bodies, Belisarno asked for Agantia's help and together they stripped the soldiers of all their clothes and weapons. Deciding that the cave was as good as any place to hide them they secreted the weapons about the ledges and the clothes they tied in a bundle and pushed them right to the back of the cave where the height of it was only two hand spans. Agantia worked quietly and methodically with Belisarno, averting her eyes from the naked bodies but otherwise showing no sign of distress. Then one by one the Trinovante loaded the men onto his shoulders and carried them to the edge of the river, leaving Agantia, in possession of her weapons again, to stand guard for him. Once he had them at the bank of the river that bordered the forest, he rolled them into the icy cold water and let the fast running current hurtle them downstream, dashing them off the rocks as they went. Agantia had told him about the water fall further down the river and Belisarno hoped that they would reach it unseen and then be smashed to pieces on the rocks. He knew that there would be search parties sent to look for the soldiers when they did not return to their fort at Rigodunum and he wanted nothing to lead back to Agantia or her family.

They returned to the cave and Belisarno fetched water and bathed Agantia's cut on her forehead and washed the blood spatters from her arms and legs. She winced and shrank from him when he touched her legs but he ignored her reaction and asked for her healer's bag of herbs to find something to put on the cut to stop infection. They decided between them that Belisarno would return and tell the settlement that he had seen her and she was all right as long as she promised him she would not take her own life. They also decided that nothing would be said about either the rape or the killings, he warned her that her mother had seen Bodua in a dream and had seen Agantia dead and so she must think of some explanation for that. He asked that she speak in council to be his dreamer when he petitioned them.

"You still want me to be your dreamer after all that has happened?"

133

"Of course. Unless you want to be a warrior now? Having killed two of the enemy you would have the right."

Agantia shook her head vigorously, "No, never!"

"Well, that settles it, you shall be my dreamer and I can look out for you so that anything else that comes to light we will deal with as and when it does, agreed?"

Agantia nodded her assent, relieved that the young warrior intended taking care of both her and the situation .

Helping her to keep her mind off what had happened, he set her the task of replenishing wood for the fire. He disappeared down to the river bank with his spear only to return with two very large fish He insisted he would cook and she must eat for it had been three days she had been fasting, and he was concerned that she was weak and still in shock from all that had happened to her. They ate their meal together in companionable silence. When it was time for him to leave her, she gulped the tears back, she couldn't show him how frightened she was at the prospect of spending another night in the forest, but he had sensed her fear, and gathered her to him and held her there for a few minutes, feeling her heart beating fast he asked if she was sure that this is what she wanted to do and she replied firmly that it was. He brushed her forehead with his lips in the gentlest of kisses and left her at the mouth of the cave.

He hurried back to the settlement, knowing that Belboudiko would be worried. He skirted the forge making sure it was only inhabited by the Smith and his family. Belboudiko who had been trying not to assume the worst was relieved to see the Trinovante and said so. Belisarno told the story as he had promised Agantia he would. How it had taken him a while to find her and how she looked as if she might have fallen for she had a cut on her head, but she was otherwise all right, and her father had been right about her hiding out in the caves. Had he known the Trinovante's prowess as a tracker Belboudiko would never have believed that it had taken so long to locate his daughter, but he was unaware of it and so believed what he was told. The relieved Smith hurried to reassure Voria that Agantia was well. Voria was relieved but there remained a niggling doubt about her daughter's safety that would disturb her sleep most of the night.

It was a larger than normal party that set out to escort the adult Agantia home after her Dark Nights. Belboudiko had been happy to accede to the Trinovante's request to ride in the parade and had insisted that he ride at his side. As before the women took the lead and Voria and Avonicca were joined by Beladora. The two dreamers were still anxious despite the Smith's assurances that Agantia was well. Beladora led the sturdy Welsh Cob that her stepdaughter normally rode and Dago the hound ran ahead of them anxious to be first to greet his mistress. They reached the place they had left her three days before and halted the horses. The dawn mist hadn't cleared and a light drizzle was beginning to fall. The breath from the horses rose in the still air and joined the mist. Several other hounds as well as Dago foraged around in the undergrowth trying to pick up a scent. People talked casually just to pass the time. Belisarno the Trinovante held his own counsel, although he felt himself grow uneasy as each moment passed without sight of Agantia. Had she held her nerve? Had she kept her promise not to take her own life? He shouldn't have left her, should he? Damn them and their ceremonies he thought. His mount caught his unease and began to paw the ground restlessly which, in turn seemed to upset some of the other horses. There was a feeling of general unrest.

Suddenly a shout went up and Dago who had scented his quarry had set off into the forest barking a welcome. At the back of the women Belisarno strained his eyes to see the first sight of her. He saw her running through the trees with the hound barking joyously at her side. Her cloak pinned high on the shoulder by his gift of the lovely owl silver brooch streamed out behind her and as she came nearer he caught the glint of the green and gold of her torcs. She finally came to a halt in front of the women and was enveloped in their grateful welcome. Everyone was talking at once, hugging and kissing her. Belboudiko smiled at the Trinovante and rode off to join the mêlée. He left Belisarno, aloof from the family gathering which, gave him an opportunity to compose his feelings and settle his face into a mask of friendly politeness.

Agantia was helped up onto her horse and she clattered by him swept along by her father's horse and the other female riders. He couldn't catch her glance and had to content himself in bringing up the rear with the rest of the men and boys. When they reached the settlement and drew up in front of the round house where the Grandmother was waiting to greet them; Belisarno was able to manoeuvre his horse nearer to hers. Their eyes met and he smiled and nodded at her trying to reassure her wordlessly that everything would be all right. He was rewarded by a small smile in return and that was sufficient for him. At a signal from the Grandmother, silence fell upon the gathering.

"Agantia, Dreamer of the Brigante we welcome you back from your Dark Nights."

"Thank you Grandmother."

"Did you abide by the rules of the Dark Nights and spend the time alone and not helped by another living being?"

Agantia paused and then in a strong, determined tone re-replied, "Yes Grandmother."

Belisarno, watching the ceremony felt suddenly saddened. This was her first lie and there would be more lies, there always were. You told the first lie, then you had to tell another lie to cover it up and so it went on until you became a practised liar. He did not want that for Agantia, he did not want her to have the same fate as his. He sighed and saw Avonicca watching him. He would have to watch that one, he knew she didn't like him, he had heard her call him Scarface which didn't bother him, but her accusation that he was a spy for the Romans was too close to the truth for comfort.

Author's Notes on Names and their meanings

1. NAMES and relationships

AGANTIA = means silver, a Brigantian girl and dreamer aged 14.

BELBOUDIKO = means strong bringer of victory, warrior and father to Agantia.

BELADORA= means strong, adored one, warrior and wife to Belboudiko, stepmother to Agantia.

VORIA = means dawn, dreamer and mother to Agantia.

AVONICCA = means of the river, dreamer and lover to Voria.

RIGANMELTA = means queen/woman of lightning, dreamer, senior elder of the tribe, Grandmother to Agantia and mother to Voria.

LUKO = means wolf, warrior of the Carvetii

BELISARNO = means strong iron, warrior of the Trinov-antes moved north when his land had been conquered by the Romans.

2. TRIBES

Brigantes – Large tribe in the North of England, taking in Yorkshire, parts of Lancashire and all the way up to Hadrian's wall in the East.

Carvetii – An off shoot of the Brigantes, occupied what is now modern day Cumbria

Trinovantes – A tribe that had originally been part of the Catuvellauni, their centre was modern day Colchester where following the Roman invasion of 43AD, the Romans had installed a colony of her retired soldiers.

3. PLACES

Rigodunum = Castleshaw near Oldham where the original Roman ruins sparked off this story.

The Island of Mona = the Isle of Anglesey

4. This story came about from reading about the Roman ruins at Castleshaw and the report that in the sixties, three young people claimed that a Roman Centurion on horse-back came charging over the fields at full pelt and rode straight through their parked up van and disappeared out the other side! The report does not say if these people were under the influence of strong drink or drugs, but the idea for the story took off in my mind!

Carolina de la Cruz

Jane stood looking at the new church, risen like a phoenix from the demolished bricks and mortar of the previous Hollins Methodist church, situated towards the end of Millgate.   She thoughtfully walked on and sat down on the low concrete wall that surrounds the planted foliage on each side of the path. This leads people on to Pit Hills. Her memory slipped back and she saw herself walking down Millgate.   The neatly laid out front gardens and semi-detached houses on Swallow Street and surrounding area became rows of terraced two up two down cottages.

Walking down Millgate she pressed the latch on the old green back gate which took her into a back yard shared by three cottages. As was the norm in this two up two down area all three shared one tippler toilet complete with cleaning rota. Each cottage did have its own coal place to feed the open fires. The opposite end from the back gate led into a large reclaimed timber yard, owned for a time by Jane's grandparents Eric and Alice Black. The cottage fronts came onto Hollins Road looking down towards the Hollinwood area. Jane lived in the middle of the cottages and next door to her lived Amy and James Jones with their daughter Freda. Theirs was the last cottage before the wood yard.   James owned the local barber's shop and kept a smallholding at the back of the premises, just lower down than the timber yard.

Jane lived with her mother and father Elsie and Walter Black. Walking in at the back door she heard her mum shout from upstairs, "Our Jane, just nip down to the butcher's, luv, will you and get us some chops for our tea. Get change out of the tin."
"Right mum."
All three cottages were surrounded with individual wood-

en paling fencing. She slipped out of the front door, stepping out of the small garden type front onto the pavement of busy Hollins Road.

At teatime the traffic and people steadily built up. There were mill workers coming home after long weaving days, occasionally pit workers from the Oak Colliery coming off shift. Jane walked on down and saw Freda from next door just coming home from the mill.

"Hiya, Freda, see you later; just going to the shop for mi mum."

As she passed the wood shop she could hear the monotonous 'chop chop chopping' from the machines that made the wood into fire lighters for people to light their open fires. Jane's grandfather, who was apparently given the nick name of 'Billy Two Sticks', endlessly turned out sticks bound together with wire. Once these were made it was up to Walter (Jane's father) to deliver the sticks to the various customers and businesses. Alas he was often the worse for drink and caused endless problems for his father.

Walking down Jane passed the barber's shop. James, the barber was often asked by his steady customers, "Have I come in here for a cut or a gossip, lad?" She called in and shouted 'hello' to James. It was a long, oblong shop with three quarters of the space taken up with a dark brown, longish, old, well worn, leather settee. In front of this were the barber's chairs. James was a man of stature, if only in size, always thinking he was right.

One morning there was a lot of shouting going on outside the three cottages. Jane stepped out to see what all the fuss was about. James was beside himself with indignation. Jane, trying her best to stifle a grin, said, "What's wrong,

James?" He was nearly jumping up and down face going redder and redder, somewhere betwixt self pity and childish rage. Now it was very rare that he called his wife, Amy, by her Christian name. So to anyone that would listen to the shouting he continued, "Do you know what Jones did last night? Woke me up she did and asked me to move over in bed. Well I ask you, what do you think about that?"

"You took all the bed. What do you expect me to do?" said Amy with a calm that can only come from someone used to dealing with the spoilt, self indulgent men of the time, (and there were many).

Amy was a lady of many talents. She could sew. When it was time for Jane needing scotch plaid kilts for school she would make them up after Jane's mum, Elsie, had bought the material from what they used to call the Dam Head Mill in Saddleworth. She looked after the poultry in the smallholding at the back of the barber's shop, often being seen taking down a bucket with the food for the hens. She would also take James's breakfast, mid-morning break, dinner and mid-afternoon break all wrapped in greaseproof paper. She was a true farmhouse cook and it was very rare that you saw her cooking in the stove. She cooked with the oven beside the open fire, where she made stews in a very blackened large pan on top of the fire. She made the best parkin Jane ever tasted and Christmas cakes, the icing beautifully made and decorated. Amy was also the person at Christmas who dispatched the poultry. All was taken in her stride.

All three cottages needed to keep a cat because of the wood shop containing a lot of mice seeking a warm place to live. Jane and Freda, living next door to each other, became more like sisters, Freda being the older of the two. One day when Jane was in Freda's house their cat was not well, so Amy said to both girls, "Go down to the shop, will you, and get a tin of cat food." This they did. Upon return they found the cat had gone; Amy had seen it off in their absence. Like the hens she had dispatched it with the farmer type, no nonsense mind, her words were, "It was suffering."

Jane's mum Elsie had a very strong personality; she had no option with Walter, Jane's father, to contend with. Walter was a frequent visitor to the various public houses in the area and there were many; some still remain to this day. At the Victoria, often called 'the Vic' by the local people, the landlady was equally well known at that time, often being seen while Jane was on her way to school, polishing the brass at the large front door as the dray man rolled the barrels down the cellar. The White Heart just higher up than the Victoria was another place that Jane's father found home from home. One night Jane's mum had run out of change for the meter (it was all slot meters then for electricity and gas). She knocked on the door of the White Heart and asked if the landlord could give her change. He was not pleased about this. Elsie soon put him in his place and said, "Well Walter's kept you going for long enough so I'm only asking for some of the change he's put in here." It was only change she wanted. Elsie worked at a school canteen when school meals were made on the premises. She also went cleaning on a Saturday afternoon.

Jane's grandfather seemed to have somewhat of a roving eye for the ladies much to Alice his wife's, and Flora his daughter's, disgust. This caused a lot of inner family turmoil at home and in Jane's house. There, there was another problem too; one day after Walter had been out all night, he did not return the following day and was not seen again. There were a lot of rumours going around the area as to his whereabouts. What remained was the fact that life became

142

much easier for Jane and her mother Elsie; they seemed to progress to better times.

Hollins Road around Millgate was a community within a larger community. Towards the Oak Colliery pit you had a barber's, a mixed food business, a butcher's, a paper shop, and a chip shop selling the best fish, chips and mushy peas around. And there was work for people to go to.

This area had its fair share of personalities. Just across the road from Jane was a shop. The owner, old Jack, sold anything but food items. He would take any coupon and knock it off the price, whatever goods you bought. There was Hadfield that would just pop into anyone's house at any time and no one seemed to mind. He had a fascination with elastic bands that he kept lovingly in a small tin box and would constantly twirl them round and round

Long silent voices all now passed into history; the only voice for those now passed is the people left that remember. Activity and life now seem replaced by quiet and grass verges. Slowly Jane started to feel more at ease as though someone was standing at her side with their arm round her shoulder. She looked round; there was no one there. Her mind started to come back to the present. The smart houses and newly built church came back into focus, although she could not understand this feeling. Sitting thinking she realized it was the anniversary of Elsie's death; she had been to the cemetery to put some flowers on her grave that morning. At that realization the sensation left her. This made her thoughtful. Could it have been the past saying 'Thank you for remembering'? Jane got up and walked slowly towards the bus stop and left the area.

Author's Note

The changes around Millgate have been many. Hollins Methodist Church at one time dominated the old fashioned two up, two down cottages. It has been put to good use for many sections of the community. Although now, a new modern church building, it still remains an essential part of the overall community. Where the Oak Colliery once stood , we now have Pit Hills. Wide green open space; this can only be a good thing. To people that lived in the area when the mills, colliery and shops were at their height; it can seem at times, quiet and remote. Nevertheless it still remains Hollinwood, friendly, helpful, and open to change.

Carol Marie Higgins

THE PIPER

The old mill loomed over the junction as it had for a century. The grime encrusted windows rhythmed the black walls as it stood there empty, forbidding.

For years rumour had it that it would be demolished; 'not before time' was the popular response. Then one day the men had moved in with lorries and scaffolding, crowbars and pickaxes, donkey jackets, wellies and bobble hats.
First the roof disappeared; what was left of the slates and the lead after decades of theft, then the window frames were removed; the smell of wood smoke marked their passing.

The work was well underway by the day that Jim Kirwin trudged home in the early morning twilight one November day. He had just finished the 10 till 6 at the mill. He hated the night shift, especially on days like this when there were no buses and the rags of mist gave warning of the fog that had been threatened on the weather forecast.

At least, he mused, Lizzie would have egg and bacon ready and possibly a potato cake if there was any mash left from last night's tea. He was a lucky man. He'd landed the girl of his dreams and she was a good cook too, a brilliant manager of their money and a loving mum to their two little girl. This morning she would have got up, stirred the fire back to life and put the kiddies' vests and liberty bodices and what not to warm on the fire guard as she always did, so they could get dressed in the warm on the rug in front of the fire instead of on the cold lino of the freezing bedroom. She was a good one, his Lizzie.

Bill, his brother, teased him that he only had the two girls whereas Bill had three strapping lads. So what! They'd plenty of time; not that he wasn't happy with his girls, mind. He adored them. And he wasn't one to call family, but if he had to choose between his Lizzie and the girls and Bill's Janey and their three boys it was no contest. That Janey, well, as Lizzie said, it takes all sorts.

As he turned the corner a strange, high-pitched note pierced his ear. He looked up, startled, aware, as always, of the bulk of the old mill on his right. He could see the grey sky through the window spaces now the roof had gone. The note came again from up the road. He turned that way. A figure caught his eye.

To say it was fantastic was an understatement. The man was tall, at least six foot six and he was standing, balancing easily, on the stone wall that surrounded the greasy waters of the old mill lodge. His trousers flapped in the breeze, one leg yellow, one a glowing scarlet. Above that was a loose tunic. Above the yellow leg it was red with a yellow sleeve, above the red leg, yellow with a red sleeve. On his head was a yellow hat banded with red. The floppy point hung over his right shoulder. He smiled at Jim as he lifted his pipe to his lips.

Again came the eerie, compelling note, then the piper began to play. His music was wild and demanding, high and sweet. Jim listened, entranced. Then he noticed the tarmac ripple. He looked more closely. From the mill came wave after wave of rats; a river of rats pouring across the road. The few vehicles around at that hour were forced to stop. Jim saw the drivers and other passers by staring in revulsion at the rats. No one spared the piper a glance.

The piper paused for breath, smiled at Jim again and raised

146

a hand in an informal salute, then leapt gracefully down the far side of the wall, playing his otherworldly melody. The rats followed him as though drawn by a magnet. Jim ran to the wall and looked over. The other was dancing over the water. As Jim watched he reached the far side. At that moment the rising sun shone briefly through the cloud and caught the gleam of colour as the piper raised and waved his strange cap. Then he was gone from sight.

Author's note

I have been told by two reliable witnesses that when the old mill at the bottom of Ripponden Road was demolished, one morning early, the rats streamed out towards Vulcan Street in a sort of living river.

Peggy Bottomley

SATURDAY WITH UNCLE

In the 1950s, unusually, my mother worked, six days a week. Fortunately for the three of us we also had a lot of family back-up – grandma, great aunt, uncle and aunt were the front line. As the eldest I often spent Saturday with my Uncle George.

My parents and uncle had a business which combined building services with a hardware shop. By the time I was seven or eight years old the shop was by far more important. Uncle (and aunty and grandma) lived next door, so most Saturdays we set off together at around half past eight. It wasn't far. Four pence bought both our bus tickets.

The shop was a rambling Victorian building. Three shops had been knocked into one. The front parts of the ground floor each still had a separate entrance and each was either show room or shop. Partitioned off, in the middle section, was an office. At the back was an enormous garage with plenty of space round the parking area for the lorry, a well-equipped carpenter's workshop and storeroom with benches, a circular saw and shelves to the ceiling. The third part was less defined and was, at one period, used as a coffin maker's workshop.

Rickety stairs led down to the huge cellars, each lit by one naked light bulb and full of wood and of things that 'will come in useful'. Upstairs were three enormous, lofty rooms, with high, cobwebby windows, each of them full with a puzzling array of lumber. The only lavatory was reached through the coffin maker's, which made a normal function into an eerie ordeal for a seven year old! The only tap, cold water of course, was in the workshop at a tiny triangular sink.

It was impossible to heat. The only warm place was the little office; this was small enough for the aged paraffin heater to keep cosy, if smelly, so, on the whole, we stayed there unless summoned by the shop bell.

What did I do in this grimy, masculine paradise? To start with I tidied and cleaned the office and mopped the floor both there and, sometimes, in the shop. I brewed up pots of strong, sweet tea for the two of us. I learned to answer the phone correctly. I sometimes served in the shop.

I sold bundles of oily wood and firelighters, Tilley lamps and the paraffin to go in them, carefully pumped up and measured by the quarter pint into bottles. That was not yet illegal. There were pencils, nails, screws, tools, paint, dishes, pans, tiles, dusters and quantities of small necessities. As instructed I kept meticulous records so that when mum came in she could 'do the books'.

And I learned. I was fascinated by the antique typewriter and started to teach myself to type on it. Also there was the workshop full of tools. I was taught how to use all of them, the saws and hammers, chisels, screwdrivers, planes and the axes. In slack periods I'd chop up scrap wood and make it into wired bundles and set it to soak up paraffin. This was the preferred firelighter in those days before the Clean Air Act.

Dinnertime arrived and would lead to earnest discussion. Did we want meat and potato, steak and kidney or cheese and onion pie? And what cake - a vanilla, a custard or a jam slice? Once the decision was made I would set off up the road to the shop. Yes it was a main road, and a busy one at that. And I had to cross it. In those days that was normal.

We ate in the office in the warm paraffin scented fug. We

drank more tea then uncle cleaned out his pipe, filled it and lit it. It was never simple; it was always fascinating. And we chatted in contented companionship.

Shortly after dinner Mum arrived as this was her time for doing the accounts. Once she had finished with the books uncle and I sneaked away for our anticipated treat. We went to change our books at the library.

The library was about half a mile away and, for us, the walk there was a delicious expedition full of ritual. By choice we went by way of the back streets and alleys. We passed long terraces of houses with donkey-stoned front steps (we had probably sold the stones if they hadn't come from the rag and bone man) and starched, white curtains half way up the sash windows. How on earth, I ask myself now, did those women manage so much whiteness in a town full of factories and coal fires? We commented, always, on the revolting but fascinating odour from the 'hide, skin and fat place'.

We talked; we always talked, about anything and everything. Uncle George was a passionately political man with a deep interest in history and gardening. He had no silly ideas about some subjects being too grown up for children; if you were old enough to walk to the library with him, you were old enough for adult conversation; this he took for granted.

His book bag contained good novels, history and biography. Mine may, from time to time, have held a school story, but was more likely to have Rudyard Kipling, Mary Renault, Rosemary Sutcliffe, Geoffrey Trease or any book on mythology or legend or history.

As we walked and talked, we watched and observed, and commented on everything around us. The patch of dandelions in a crack in the pavement, the bubbles of tar melting between the cobbles on the street; nothing was too ordinary to escape our attention.

We arrived; we separated; each busy about personal interests. We met again at the desk, newly laden with the next week's reading. Then we went upstairs to the museum and art gallery. Sometimes my sister was with us. I treasure the memory of putting her in the stocks at the top of the stairs. Where are they now? Then there was Epstein's bust of Churchill (one of uncle's heroes) to admire.

Finally there was a tour of our favourites. To begin with was the glass case with the Chinese clothes. We marvelled regularly over the tiny silk shoes and shuddered as uncle explained them. We wondered over the glorious eighteenth century glassware; the wine glasses with the air-twist stems, and the walking sticks. Then there were the pictures. Some stand out. We loved the two rosy girls under the briar bush and the dark-skinned lady draped in cream and pink and puzzled over the enigmatic title 'Corner of the Talmud School'.

And then went back and, shortly after, caught the bus home. It was not everybody's ideal Saturday. But we learned a lot.

Author's note

These are memories from childhood.

Marjory Travis

"D..a..a..a..d".

The word danced on my tongue. I used that elongated sing song tone all too familiar to my parents, indicating that I wanted something.

The reply was in a questioning, authoritative, flat tone. "Yes?"

The fact that my father answered in the affirmative was not an indication of pre-empted approval to whatever I was about to ask, it was simply his first line of defence. I was in my early teens and had mastered the art of listening to those three letters being spoken, and had developed an uncanny ability to read his mood and execute the line of strategy required. Sometimes I asked, adding hurriedly in the same breath, as if somehow the quicker I said it the less of a fabrication it actually was, that Mum had said "Yes". Clearly the only thing Mum had said was "Go and ask your Father". This applied vice versa and often involved many trips between parents, relaying misinterpreted messages, albeit with ever so slight a variance on the spoken word, from one to another. When necessary I resorted to other well honed tactics that usually worked in my favour. Interrupting him, with glasses perched precariously on the end of his nose and with both being pointed in the direction of a western paperback or calling out while he was digging in the far corner of the vegetable garden. Asking the obvious, "Are you reading?" or "Are you digging the garden Dad?" and reporting back to Mum that "Dad said yes" was indeed downright naughty, however not considered by me to be an actual falsehood. It was merely a case of a strong willed teenager, faced with parental procrastination, making the decision for them. Tried and trusted methods required a greater degree of patience and perseverance by me. I would follow my father around while he dug for worms, sitting beside him while he wound catgut line onto the reel, selected the right hooks and packed the well used and smelly bag. He would attempt to get rid of me by asking me to thread a worm onto the hook. I was revolted by the whole procedure but the entire time I chattered incessantly. Annoyingly so. Then just as he was heading out the door I'd ambush him with my question. It worked religiously. Nothing stood between my father and fishing. The peace and quiet of the river bank must have been a blessed relief.

This time my request was simple and as I stood on the chair, reaching into the highest cupboard, I promised that "Yes" I will look after it, "Yes" I will put it back and "No" I won't lose any pieces. It sat on the jars of jam, pickles and preserved fruit, this prized treasure of a man who coveted or kept so few worldly possessions. Atop the cream of the crop, the position in the cupboard was a representation of its worthiness. It was undoubtedly the most beautiful thing. I cleared a large space on the green laminated kitchen table, unrolled the accompanying map of the finished product, placed the sugar bowl on the top left corner, a jar of homemade blackberry jam on the far right and various condiments around the edges to keep it from reverting rapidly to its previous shape. I tipped the contents of the plastic bag onto the table. Curling my ankles around the chrome chair legs I looked at the clutter before me and as I searched for the first clues of semblance I become lost in the challenge. I became lost in time.

"Not another letter? You only wrote to him yesterday". I looked up. I had been so engrossed in what I was doing that I hadn't heard my father come into the kitchen. "I'm just writing to tell him that the trip is organised. I've just received a letter from the merchant shipping company. I've been accepted as a passenger. It's quite some trip Dad, the ship even goes through the Panama Canal. It's going to take nearly 4 months to get to England".

As usual I had all but covered every inch of the table. One half appeared more orderly, letters received and ready to be posted, legal paperwork in neat piles, all representing my life and the untrodden path, creating nerves and excitement in unison. On the other half of the table was my fathers treasure and whilst appearing the messiest, was no longer a challenge, coming together as a whole many times over the years, calming and a joy to behold when completed. I had surrounded myself with plans for the future and a com-forting reassurance from the past and I alternated between the two. As I reached for the letter of importance I noticed the direction of his eyes fall to the other side of the table.

"Yes, I'll put it back" I said rather tiredly, predicting the comment on the tip of his tongue.

"Make sure you do", he said, the tone more authoritative than necessary.

He picked up the letter and read through it.

"Seems like a long way to go to marry someone. Must be pretty special this bloke from Limeside".

I changed the subject quickly to avoid being teased about the love of my life.

"Where are you off to?" I asked, noticing that he had his old fishing clothes on.

The smell seemed to permeate the room but I had long outgrown being disgusted by the aroma. It had been a part of my life for near on twenty one years now.

"The dam up on the Cape" he replied.

"Can I come" I asked.

"If you can shut up long enough to let the fish bite, then yes". These were fair comments. I had been barred long ago from most hunting and fishing trips due to the fact that silence was a prerequisite to catching anything. Now I was soon to embark on a new life and a few hours fishing with my father seemed like a nice way to spend an afternoon.

I pulled an old pair of his overalls on and checked that there was a bag of sweets in the glove box of the car just in case there was nothing biting and we stayed for more hours than I thought necessary. At least then I could listen to the radio and eat mints. But this time I didn't get bored. Today the trip was more about checking the growth of the fingerlings from the Salmon Ponds that my father had stocked the dam with than catching anything. We hooked fish and my father checked their size and health then threw them back. He slipped on the mud and frightened the life out of me when he couldn't get out of the water, I fell in trying to rescue him. As usual I snagged the line umpteen times. He got annoyed, I laughed. I got annoyed, he laughed. We kept one good sized fish for Pop and talked all the way home.

I was listening to records in my room a few days later when my father came in and sat on the bed.

"We don't want you to go. Your mother and I don't want you to go to England". Ever so gently and ever so quietly. No permission had been asked, no refusal had been given. No game between parent and child had been played.

And so it lay on the table before me. Everything that should have pieced together effortlessly, everything that had been as bright and colourful in my mind as the unfurled map, all now a complete shambles. I put the letter into the envelope and swept the contents on the other side of the table into the plastic bag and threw it into the cupboard. I had finished one thing and not the other. The big picture had become much bigger than I could ever have anticipated.

The combined aroma of sweet and sour wafted out as the door opened and I momentarily hesitated. The house was now on the market and this was the last cupboard to be emptied. The process of clearing out had been quite a journey, an emotional mixture much the same as that which I now inhaled. I stacked the jars and bottles on the stove below, reading labels as I did so, recognising my mother's handwriting. Plum Jam 2005. Still making jams and sauces till the end I observed. The plum tree my father had planted before he died had kept her busy for well over three decades, as if somehow he had known they would need each other. Flinching initially as my fingers touched something that had fallen behind the last row of bottles, I soon felt a warm wave of familiarity. "Yes, I will look after it" I happily declared.

It was time for a break anyway and as I sipped the hot coffee I observed the contents of the bag spilled before me. "Where do I start?" I asked myself, keen to commence this welcome walk down memory lane. Some time later and boiling the jug for the third time, more out of frustration this time than need, I once more climbed up onto the chair, standing on my tip toes. Tighten the screws before the chattels sale, I made a mental reminder to myself as the timber chair wobbled beneath me. Searching yet again, I became annoyed that it seemed more important now than ever to find it and thinking that there couldn't possibly be a piece missing. It must be here somewhere. "Where is it?" I yelled, the words echoing in the near empty house.

"I kept your letters" he said. He held a bundle of airmail envelopes, each one fattened with declarations of love, tied together with a red ribbon, a bow keeping memories intact. My letters. Addressed to Limeside, the address I knew by heart. It all seemed surreal. Someone had turned the clock back and he was exactly as I remembered him, standing before me, here in the place I had dreamed about, the place I had yearned for. I sorted the letters into chronological order from the postmarks and started to read.

It was a journey into my past and the future I had meticulously planned 36 years before. As I neared the end of the bundle, the big trip became the focus of each letter. "My passport and visa arrived today", one letter proclaimed. "I've had my inoculations, smallpox hurt", I wrote in another. It was all so excitingly imminent. The end of my rainbow was Oldham. "I've just been fishing with Dad up on Table Cape". I re-read the words and laughed at the description of our day. I remembered it as if it were yesterday and treasured holding a written memory of my father. It took months for me to open the next letter for I, better than anyone, knew what was to come. I started to put it back in the envelope, wondering how one letter could produce so many tears, for surely a thousand had been cried and many times over. Noticing something inside the envelope I tipped it upside down onto the table. And there it was, lying before me. One single thing, so small and seemingly insignificant on its own, recognisable only to someone who knew it so well. Accidentally sealed inside, caught up in the mayhem of the decision making all those years ago, across the other side of the world. A message from my father. As if somehow he had known that we would find each other again. "No, I won't lose any pieces" I whispered.

Author's Note

My father had patiently collected tokens from the Shell Petrol Station and the jigsaw puzzle and accompanying map was a limited edition. It outlined Australia, surrounded by sea, each state and territory covered with flora, animals, reptiles and butterflies unique to that area. There are now 999 pieces in Tasmania and one piece in Oldham.

Faye Burgess

SNOW

In a way it was the silence that woke her, silence you could feel. Chrissie opened her eyes and poked her nose from under the blankets. Cold stung the inside of her nostrils and the light that seeped through the gap between the curtains was curiously grey.

She slid out of bed, being careful to place her feet on the sheepskin rug rather than on the wooden floor, shrugged on her dressing gown and felt for her slippers. She opened the curtain a bit more and found the window a frozen tracery of ferns and leaves. She pressed her nose to the glass and then stood back to examine the two holes left by her breath. She raised her eyes and saw the thick white flakes falling implacably.

Snow! A thrill of excitement coursed through her. Snow; the first snow of the winter and with it the promise of snowballs, snowmen, sledging. A kaleidoscope of ideas and plans flashed through her head. She ran downstairs.

Her parents were talking quietly over a cup of tea. Dad was in his work trousers and two jumpers. He was lacing up his heavy boots and his thick overcoat was over the back of a chair. Her mother handed her a cup and she listened carefully.

Dad had already checked. There was thick snow well up above the level of the doorstep. There were no buses. The snow was being driven by a high wind. He, dad, could probably get to the shop, but none of the others stood a chance. There would be no school today in any case – in fact if you were small going out would be dangerous. So they would stay in. There was enough food for a day or two and as soon as the wind dropped things would be easier. He pulled on his coat, added a cap and scarf and left. She watched him as he hunched out of sight towards the main road.

Susie, Chrissie's little sister sidled in, moaning about the cold. They ate breakfast and dressed quickly; vest and liberty bodice, socks and blouse, dungarees and the cardies mum had knitted and then settled down to a day confined to the house. There were books, comics and jigsaws, there was paint and crayons and sticky shapes to make patterns on paper, there were dominoes and draughts and the radio for 'Listen with Mother' and music. The Wooden Tops were on the television because it was Friday. There were dolls and the shop. There were, inevitably squabbles and tears. There was 'helping mum'. Then, after tea, there was bath and bed.

Saturday saw more of the same. The snow fell with a relentless viciousness. The two little girls gazed uselessly out of the window at the blank white. They heard the wind roaring round the eaves. They sighed and went back to their interrupted play.

On Sunday the sun shone on a frozen world. The wind had whipped the snow into curling waves in front of the house and it all sparkled as if bejewelled. There was no way they could walk the half mile to church but with care and Wellington boots, bonnets, scarves and mittens they could go out and riot across the lawn flinging balls of glorious white at each other in cheerful battle then, in a sudden truce, rolling a big ball to make a giant snowman.

They charged in, ravenous for dinner with glowing cheeks, frozen hands and chapped lips. Afterwards they slept, curled like puppies on the old, red settee.

"Come on, you two lazybones, I've got the sledge."

Susie squealed with excitement and they both ran to collect their outside clothes that had dried on the rail in front of the stove.

Dad had cleared a path to the gate and they followed him up the road to the tree-lined lane that led to the fields. They struggled manfully with the snow, singing Good King Wenceslas at the tops of their voices.

The meadow lay before them, a pristine sparkling sheet. Chrissie stepped, tentatively at first, then with growing bravado, screaming with laughter at the guilty pleasure of being the first to mar the white perfection. Dad smiled too as the weariness of the last few days faded a little from his eyes. He pulled the heavy wooden sledge to the top and loaded up his daughters, the littlest in front, gave them careful instructions and a judicious push.

The sledge edged forwards then gathered pace down the slope and slid easily to the bottom, the two little girls shrieking with merriment all the way. They pulled the sledge back to the top, arriving pink-cheeked and bright-eyed. They slid again and again, chuckling with mounting glee.

In less than half an hour the noise had attracted others and soon the long slope was alive with bright knitted bonnets, balaclavas, scarves and mittens and the sound of a dozen children intent on vigorous enjoyment and of their parents chatting and laughing in neighbourly accord.

Too soon the sun began to sink and the cold struck. Too soon the laughing throng became aware of damp clothes and snow in boots. Too soon one of the youngest children began to cry with cold, discomfort and tiredness.

As the gold shaded to red in the sky the adults loaded their children on to the sledges and started to pull them down the lane to home and warm and soup and hot chocolate – and to dreams of tomorrow.

Author's note

In 1954 we were snowed in for several days and once we could go out we had memorable games in the snow. Fortunately photographs of both the games and the snow still exist to form a good basis for a bit of embroidery.

Maggie Nicholson

A SPOONFUL OF SUGAR

Maire Reagan cancelled the buzzer, checked the perfection of her chignon in the window's inky black reflection and went to give the mithering patient whatever it was she wanted.

Maire had worked as a nursing carer at St. Stephen's Old People's Home for four years now and she was two weeks short of her 50th birthday. During her time at the home she had seen and known hundreds of patients: some had come there to give their relations a break from the constant need for nursing; others had come to spend their final weeks, months, or sometimes years in the peaceful and secure surroundings of the home.

When Maire responded to the buzzer, Stanley had stayed where he was on the rest couch, which was provided for night staff in the small rest room next to the nurses' station. He pulled the sheet over his bare middle. There wasn't much chance of anyone coming into the room but you never knew. Maire and Stanley had been lovers now for ten of the thirteen months that Stanley had worked at the home.

She had been attracted to him from the start, as he was everything her husband wasn't. When Maire had married George he had been young, vibrant, loving and had had a full head of hair. Their twenty-nine year old marriage had taken its toll; George's looks had gone, and in bed Maire could only describe him as caring, gentle and kind. Stanley, on the other hand, was hard, rough, devilishly good-looking, and merely used Maire for his own pleasure. This form of love, if that was the word for it, excited and satisfied Maire in a way that George's attentions had never done.

Maire could not cover her irritation at Lillian Geek's

request for assistance to go to the toilet.

"Why didn't you go before you went to bed?" she had barked. Maire didn't even listen to the answer. She was desperate to get back to Stanley and said nothing more as she bundled the 87-year old Lillian back into bed. Before Maire went back to Stanley on the couch she switched Lillian's bedroom light off and banged the door closed behind her. She knew Lillian was afraid of the dark but was so intent on getting back to Stanley that she forgot. Lillian spent the dark hours of the night clutching her bedclothes tightly in her fingers held under her chin, gazing into the dark room and imagining monsters in every corner. Four days later Lillian Geek died peacefully in her sleep.

Edith Carpenter and Shirley Moore had moved into St. Stephen's within a week of one another almost twelve months ago. Both had been unable to cope with the physical demands of looking after themselves at 85 and 82 respectively. But their minds were active, and they would spend their time reading, completing the crosswords in the more stretching papers, and talking about the good old days. Neither of the two ladies liked Maire Regan, but they were careful to keep it from her.

At the home, Maire's impending birthday was the topic of gossip for staff and patients alike. They were going to give her a surprise birthday party the evening prior to the actual date, since that was her last duty before a week's holiday. She was going to Benidorm. It was George's present to her, along with a pair of peach satin slippers as he wanted to have something to wrap for her. Stanley knew exactly what he was going to give Maire for her present. Maire also knew what Stanley would give her and she knew she'd like it.

A collection amongst the staff and residents at the home had raised £42 and they had bought Maire the collection of Elvis LPs she'd told them about. One or two had bought her small individual presents. Ruby Daniels had bought her a cubic zirconia brooch to match the earrings bought by Lesley Woods, the home's cook. Lesley and Maire were old friends from a previous job; Lesley had also offered to make sandwiches and a cake for the surprise party. Edith and Shirley had bought a present between them, a half-bottle of cognac. Stanley had told them it was her favourite tipple. Shirley had sneaked across the road outside St Stephen's in her slippers to the mini-market on the corner. The half-bottle had only cost £4.99, and was probably intended as cooking liquor, but it was only for Maire whom Shirley reckoned wouldn't know the difference. And after all it's the thought that counts. At the time of her death, Lillian Geek had been knitting Maire a woollen waistcoat with some lovely green wool she had unpicked from one of her own cardigans as she hadn't been able to afford to buy a gift. But Maire would never know about that now, would she?

On the day of the party, George, who was in on the surprise, had to talk Maire into getting ready early so that he could get her to St. Stephen's for 6.00 p.m. Her duty shift didn't start until 8.00 p.m. but George had made the excuse that, after dropping her off, he would have to go back into work to organize an urgent order they hadn't completed.

As he watched Maire getting dressed, carefully selecting her smartest lingerie, applying perfume to all those private pulse points, and attaching her dark silky stockings to the clasps of her suspenders, George wished he was going to be the recipient of her favours, but he doubted it. He hadn't been that lucky for almost twelve months now. George suspected that Stanley was the lucky guy. It made George's blood boil but what could he do?

Maire hadn't noticed George watching her. She was think-ing about Stanley's body and how he used it on her. The previous evening when they had again been on duty alone they had been busy and there had been no time for one of their mutually satisfying sessions. Maire had been angry that the residents had been so needy and had deprived her of time to enjoy Stanley's body. But Stanley had just laughed and told her not to worry, as he wouldn't let her go on holiday without the benefit of his very special atten-tions. She had been unable to think of anything else since.

The banner proclaiming "Happy birthday, Maire" was stretched across the nurses' station and greeted Maire as she walked through the door. It was the second thing she noticed, the first being Stanley who was looking very tasty, in her opinion, in a blue blazer and white shirt; and it explained why he was there early as well. Her first thought was that Stanley had organized the party for her but then commonsense took over and she real-ized it was probably Lesley Woods who had made the ar-rangements. She hoped the party wouldn't last too long as she simply couldn't wait to get her hands on Stanley.

Everyone greeted her with a "happy birthday" and gave her their presents. They all chatted happily and excited-ly about the occasion. The surprise party, how nice she looked, was that new perfume she was wearing? Maire enjoyed being the centre of attention but was willing the time away so that Stanley could get his hands on her.

In fact, the time did pass quickly; what with the drinks, the buffet and the presentation of her main present. Maire was genuinely pleased with her Elvis LPs and made sure everyone knew. One by one the residents bade their goodnights and were soon tucked up in bed since the day staff, who had stayed on for the party, had good-naturedly offered to help Maire and Stanley with their workload on this special night.

By 10.30 p.m. all the day staff had left, all the residents were sleeping soundly, and Maire was kissing George goodbye on the doorstep. George reminded Maire that he would be picking her up at 8.00 a.m. sharp, so that she could change before they left for the airport. She rather bad-temperedly told him she knew, and that he had better get off home and finish the packing.

George guessed what her rush was. He'd seen the looks she and Stanley had shared during the evening, and he thought he saw Stanley brush his hand across Maire's buttocks; but he wasn't sure. He told her he loved her, gave her a small kiss on the cheek that was offered to him, and returned to the car.

When Maire had seen George's car turn right on to the dual carriageway taking him home she locked the front door for the night and set the public lighting to dim, usual practice for the night duty. Stanley was waiting for her as she reached the nursing station. He was already lying on the staff rest-couch with all his clothes removed. In his left hand he held a can of beer, rescued from the bar and secreted away for himself earlier in the evening. In the other hand he held the cognac he'd talked Edith and Shirley into buying for Maire. Maire had once told him that cognac had an effect on her and tonight he intended to find out how.

When she was at home Maire liked to drink her cognac from the fat-bellied brandy glasses that she'd bought at the charity shop. They had only cost her 40 pence for the two – she'd waited till the sale - but she felt that they enhanced her enjoyment of the rich and strong liquor. Unfortunately, all she could find tonight as she checked the cupboards in the nurses' station was a dimpled high-ball glass. Maire hoped it hadn't previously contained a resident's toothbrush – or even worse - her teeth. As she clutched the glass in her left hand she decided that on a night like this she didn't care and she determinedly unbuttoned the front of her uniform with her right hand.

She sauntered over to the couch, savouring every moment and taking in every detail of Stanley's body as she did so. As she reached him, and Stanley could smell her potent perfume, he put down his un-opened can on the floor, unscrewed the top of the bottle of cognac and poured Maire a very generous helping of the silky amber-brown liquid into what appeared to him to be a denture pot. He wanted her to fizz for him tonight.

Maire stood proud and provocative before Stanley and let her uniform slip over her shoulders and slide to the floor, before taking the charged glass from him and drinking her fill. As her eyes peered over the rim of the glass she was pleased to see that Stanley clearly appreciated the combination of red satin, stockings and suspenders she had carefully put together.

For his part, Stanley had waited long enough. He reached out his arms to envelop Maire's generous body. Stanley believed that Maire's body was generous in both size and favour - just as he liked it. He let his hands wander everywhere as she drained her glass and deftly reached for the bottle to pour herself another. Maire pushed Stanley back and settled herself alongside him on the couch, lazily downing her second cognac as Stanley manoeuvred himself into position over her.

Stanley kissed her hard and tasted just a hint of the liquor she had swallowed. As Stanley began to make love to her, Maire's head began to swim. Stanley was amused when Maire described what they did together as making love - however he knew enough to realise he was on to a good thing and kept his amusement to himself.

Tonight, more than ever before, Maire's senses began to whirl at the feel of Stanley's body on hers. She was tired, but her whole body tingled at his heavy, directed touch. As Stanley moved onto and into her she was finding it hard to focus on him so she let her eyes close. His image was burned on her brain anyway and she didn't need to look. His touch and the sensual feelings it transferred to her body were all that mattered.

Stanley noticed her closed eyes and the dreamy expression her parted lips conveyed and thought proudly that he was having a greater effect on her than ever before. If Maire wanted to call this making love then Stanley was okay with that. After all, he was trying to float his boat and not rock hers. He was holding her head in his hands and he could feel her temples pulsing slow but very heavy.

As Stanley worked towards his own fulfilment, and, as a consequence, Maire's, her hands slipped from where they had been clasped on the back of his neck onto the pillow. She looked like she had raised her arms in the classic pose of surrender. As she breathed out deeply into his face the heady alcohol-tinged air from her throat mixed with the intoxicating fumes of her birthday perfume and profoundly stirred all of his senses. Stanley suspected from the looseness of her actions and the impression that she was surrendering to him, that she had reached total abandonment, and was in the process of achieving the summit of her satisfaction.

It was all he needed to ensure his own. Stanley didn't stop what he was doing for several minutes wringing every last moment of physical pleasure from their union. Sweat from the exertion had formed on both of the lovers' brows and a couple of droplets from his own fell onto Maire's face. As they rolled haphazardly, in stops and starts, down her cheeks they could almost have been tears. But the sensation did not make her react. Stanley stared at her, almost - but not quite - lovingly, and blew warm breath from his lungs, directed by his pursed lips, on to the small damp patches of both their sweat on Maire's face.

One of Maire's eyelids had slipped open half revealing the eye beneath it, and the strangeness of her look startled him. He said her name. She didn't respond. He squeezed her arm and called her name. There was no response and there wouldn't be. Unbeknown to Stanley Maire's heart had stopped and she had just died underneath him.

One week later the coroner announced that Maire Regan had died of heart failure during a strenuous bout of extra-marital sex with her lover. Before commiserating with the deceased's widower the coroner stated that, whilst unusual, the circumstances were not unique and the death would be officially described as "from natural causes".

In truth it was anything but natural. Maire Regan had been as strong as an ox and in the fullness of time would have been more likely to have seen off Stanley. However during their time at the home, Edith and Shirley had suspected, and through quiet, patient, research subsequently confirmed, that Maire Regan had single handedly disposed of seven old dears, who had either become too much trouble for her to look after and still have time for Stanley, or had irritated her with their helplessness.

169

Maire Regan had not carried out her duties with compassion, but merely quickened the exit of the nuisances in her life by taking theirs. Maire's method was simple but very effective. Mixing brandy and methadone and administering small quantities of the mixture to already incapacitated bodies had caused their hearts to slow down and stop. The effect was of a person quietly going to sleep and never waking. In old patients the effect appeared nothing but natural.

Except, that was, to Edith and Shirley, who had spent their "good old days" as nursing sisters at Boundary Park Hospital. From the day their suspicions were aroused until the day after Lillian Geek showed them the half-finished waistcoat - the day she died - they had not had the courage to do anything about it. When told of Lillian's demise they agreed there and then to avenge her.

Edith never took her methadone prescription after that day, feigning sickness and promising to take it later, and ignoring the pain for which it was prescribed. Shirley had bought the bottle of cognac from the mini-market across the road and brought it to the room they shared. Together they had both taken a celebratory tot from the bottle before they had poured the stolen medicine into it. They had re-tightened the top and stuck on the pink ribbon bow they had bought to adorn it. At that concentration it would do its job on the healthiest of individuals and yet still appear natural.

Lillian's death had upset them greatly and the thought of Maire enjoying either Stanley, or the week in Benidorm, had upset them even more. No! She had gone too far and they were going to make her pay. They were going to teach Maire a lesson she would never have the opportunity to remember. They decided to "give her a taste of her own medicine"!

Author's note
The memory of this story comes from something my Nan told me about her life in a care home, the fiction is the finished story that I came up with.

Nigel Hague

THE TRIP

Florrie Garside walked slowly into the hardware shop on Lees Road. She ached with tiredness and she was frozen. At first sight there was nobody in the shop even though the bell had rung as she went in. Then she saw the tiny figure of a very young girl behind the counter.

"Helping out in your holidays are you?" she asked kindly.

The child nodded shyly.

"What can I get you," she asked politely.

"A quarter pint of paraffin and a bundle of oily wood, please." She placed an old medicine bottle on the counter then let her mind wander while the little girl went to pump the paraffin into the measuring jug. That would go into her little Tilley lamp and would save the light when she went up to bed; a few sticks of the wood would help to light the fire. That was a treat really but it took so long without and the day it was she really did need to light the fire fast. The house got so cold while they were all out at work.

"That'll be nine pence, please."

The child had come back unnoticed and placed the filled bottle and the newspaper wrapped bundle on the counter. She carefully counted the proffered coins into the right compartments in the till drawer and wrote up the sales in the ledger.

"Is your mam Molly Walters?"

The little girl nodded.

"She was a very clever girl. We went to evening classes; she did book-keeping and got a job in the office at the mill. Very well thought of she was."

"Mummy's here now. I'll tell her that a friend has come in."

Barely a minute later Molly came through from the office followed by her daughter.

"Florrie, how lovely to see you, it's been years. Run along now, Patsy, your uncle has a job for you to do in the office. Little pitchers you know..." she added to her friend as Patsy trotted off obediently.

As Patsy had expected her mum was still talking when she came back quarter of an hour later.

"...it's not too expensive, £10 each full board, less for the children, of course. We're travelling by coach – we'll visit eight different countries and of course we'll see the play. It's a bit cheaper because we're going during Wakes, not the summer holidays. It's something I've always wanted to do and Bob and Betty are keen too."

"Mummy, I've brewed up and Daddy will be here soon."

"I'll have to dash, Florrie. Lovely to see you again."

Florrie left the shop deep in thought.

"Nice fire, Florrie. It's good to come home to a warm house." Vera, Florrie's sister held her chilled hands to the blaze.

"Oh I cheated, popped out and got a bit of oily wood.

173

Did you know that Molly Walters as was and her brother and her husband have that hardware shop on Lees Road?"

"Do they? Haven't seen either of them in years; not since they left St. Pat's. She married that Yank at the end of the war, didn't she? I wonder how that turned out; you hear stories."

"Well it seems all right. They have a lovely little girl, bright too. She served me and she had everything off. …They're going to Oberammergau to see the Passion Play in 1960. They've booked already; they got it out of the Universe. I suppose they have to save up. It'll cost them £10 each."

"Phew! That's steep. Still, if they think it's worth it…"

"I'm wondering about going too…"

"Oh, Florrie, it's not for the likes of us – and how would you manage with the foreign money and the food – not to mention not understanding a word anybody says?"

Over the next few weeks Florrie spent some time working out figures on the back of envelopes. She had to eat of course and pay her share of the rent and put her shillings in the pot on the mantelpiece where they kept the money for the meters and tip up her share of the housekeeping, but there must be some way she could save a bit. After all it was only 1957 – she'd three years to save up for the holiday and spending money and a few new dresses.

Her bus fare was 6d; three pence each way. But if she got off a stop earlier she'd save a halfpenny each journey – that was sixpence a week or £1.5s a year. Then there was tea at work; if she took cold tea in a bottle and a sandwich instead of going to the canteen that would save the same amount. £2.10s a year was a good start. It would mean she had to get up a bit earlier, but it would be worth it. Then she would see if she could save anything from her odd money. She needed her sixpence for the collection at church and tuppence for the club man, but if she got her book every other week instead of every week she would save 13/- in a year. She could arrange with her friend Hilda. If they each got the book on alternate weeks and swapped it would help them both. Hilda was always hard up.

Once her calculations and arrangements were made she looked carefully through the Universe, found the advert Molly had told her about and made a trip to the post office, bought a stamped envelope and piece of note paper and written to the travel agent, then, holding her breath at her own daring, posted the letter.

"I think you've been very silly," announced her brother, Ted. Vera, standing behind him nodded solemnly.

"It's too late now. I've booked and paid the deposit."

"So long as you don't expect us to bail you out when you get out of your depth."

Florrie could feel nervous tears starting in her eyes, but knew she had expected this and it was the reason she had rushed everything in the anonymity of the crowded post office. And she did understand them. The Workhouse had closed and was now the hospital, but the fear of it remained. She knew older people who would sooner die than go into that building whatever the doctor said.

Over the next few months Florrie had ample opportunity

to regret her impulsiveness. She made sure that she sent her nieces and nephews their normal postal order for 5/- on their birthdays. She started early to knit each a warm scarf for Christmas and that was a little saving on what she would normally have spent. She was careful to treat her brothers and sisters as she always had. The week in Blackpool at Wakes had been long planned and booked; she sent postcards as usual but for the first time did not bring back a souvenir. When she went to buy her new outfit she sighed over the clothes she saw in Buckley and Proctors, in Hardcastles and in Flacks and bought a skirt and blouse on the market. They were much cheaper and she was careful to cut out the 'Empire made' label. She almost rebelled against the self-imposed parsimony until she was re-heartened by the sight of the growing balance in her Post Office account and the realisation that she was easily able to send off the monthly postal order to the Travel Agents.

As time went on she grew accustomed to the differences in her life. She no longer went to the pictures every week but every fortnight or every month. She and Hilda started to go to the library on Saturday afternoon after work. Best of all Ted and Vera, once they realised that there was nothing much they could do and that Florrie was maintaining her contributions to the household expenses, had stopped making snide remarks and sometimes even made interested comments. She didn't go away at Wakes for two years but had little trips, to the fair on the West Street Site, to the park, and to Chew Valley.

Florrie felt her excitement rising as her holiday grew nearer. She bought clothes suitable for the warmer weather she was expecting and a light mac and wool for a cardigan in case... She applied for her passport and changed some money at the bank – so many different sorts. She split it into carefully labelled bags. Everyone was being so helpful.

Then, at last, she was off.

Author's note

I did go on a coach trip to Oberammergau with my family in 1960, so some of the memories are mine. To this I've added much that I was told about the way people lived.

Marjory Travis

UNSEASONABLE

Whit Sunday was always a rush. We got up, went to Mass, came back and ate our eggs on toast then charged off to get ready. Whit Sunday was the day for 'walking round'.

Adults simply wore their best clothes. So did boys unless they were altar boys or one of the May Queen's pageboys. Then I have to admit they were worse off than we were. Looking back it must have taken courage to process round the town in a cassock and a lacy surplice or in velvet pants and a satin blouse. However I suppose it must have taken even more courage to say 'no' to mum.

We, the girls, dressed in white. In my case this meant a straight white skirt, a shirt blouse and the plain white court shoes that I wore at no other time and that had cost 12/6d at Finnegan's. It went on, as did everything, over the roll-on that always, because I am short waisted, rolled up to the waist and nearly cut me in half. It held up my stockings and, as always, I carefully fastened the back suspender first so that my seam was straight. This worked even though one suspender button had dropped off and been replaced by an old shirt button. The younger girls, the Holy Angels, wore medals on a red ribbon and a red cloak. We, the Children of Mary, had pale blue ribbons and cloaks.

We went to Derker Street, our parish meeting place, where we found the band, the statue secure on its flower-bedecked platform and the banner. Over the next half hour more and more people arrived and we were gradually organised into formation.

Then we were off. It did not matter that it was distinctly chilly and we all had goose pimples; it did not matter that the sky was grey and threatening; this is Oldham. I don't suppose we even noticed the weather.

It was a matter of pride to march in an almost rigidly disciplined way behind the tall banner, borne by two men who carried the weight in a sort of leather holster worn over the shoulders and used their hands to steady the poles. Four other men held ropes attached to the top of the poles as a further safeguard and we girls looked pretty as we held sweet little satin ribbons also attached to the top. We worked as a team, we and the men, and relayed each other as necessary.

We were a brave sight. Down Shaw Road we went and waited for St. Anne's to go past then we followed them. All the bands played hymns loudly; unfortunately they did not always, or even usually, play the same hymns as the bands in front and behind.

The route never varied; down the Bottom of the Moor to Mumps, past Buckley and Proctors, up Rhodes Bank to Union Street. On we went, past the Victory Cinema De Luxe and the ABC and the Odeon, then the library and the Post Office, the Baths and the Lyceum. Then there was the Grosvenor Cinema and the billiard hall; Horsman's the pork butcher and the Gaumont with the entrances to the public toilets in front. By this time all the parishes had joined in and the procession circled the town centre.

We turned up George Street. It was known for being a 'brew' and it was, indeed, hard work. By coincidence my father and I were both on the banner 'team' at this stage. All was going well as we passed the Lung Wah Chinese restaurant, famed in those days for the dead cats that the environmental health found in their fridge when chicken was on the menu.

Nowadays, with Spindles and Town Square what happened next is impossible. We, however, were ready for it. We stepped into Market Place and into the wind. Market place was vast in those days, a large, grass-covered roundabout. It was 'fed' by George Street and High Street, Manchester Street and West Street, where the huge empty patch of ground, where the fair was held at Wakes, left us exposed, Cheapside and Henshaw street and of course little Water Street, the oldest of them all. Against all logic outside Oldham the wind blew along all these roads at once, swirling round the amphitheatre of the massive junction driving scourging rain before it.

We got it in the face to begin with. Then the ribbons started to pull and we slowly wound them round our hands to avoid the ignominy of losing one. We noticed the strain on the faces of the six men who were struggling to stop the banner either flying off or come crashing down. We forgot to be pretty; that was past praying for anyway now the rain had plastered our hair against our heads, and we started to pull on the ribbons to support the efforts of the bearers.

We turned into High Street, passing blindly in front of Yates' Wine Lodge, Hardcastles, Woolworth's, and Salter's, fighting all the time to retain our balance and stabilise the banner. As we came to the iron railings and the Town Hall we knew we had won. It was going to be hard work. Nobody was going to be able to take over, that was risky, but if we went carefully we were safe.

We did get back without any drama, though everyone was rather bedraggled and most people were chilled to the bone. We were not cold though our legs were blue and our hands were numb.

Down came the banner and was rapidly rolled and stowed. In went the statue. Mums dashed over with raincoats and cardigans. And gradually we started for home. We piled into the back of the van and dad started the engine wordlessly. Off we went, uncomfortable, but out of the wind.

Mum of course had to have the last word.

"This is nothing. I remember the year it snowed."

Author's note

This really happened like this. The memory is far from misty!

Marjory Travis

George Black turned up the volume of the wireless in order to drown the noisy chimes emanating from the grandfather clock and added more coal to the range.

A train driver by profession, he was also a gifted craftsman and loved working with wood in his spare time. During the course of his life, he had made many useful and decorative objects. His hobby had begun out of necessity making useful items for his wife and family – doorstops, ironing boards, cutting boards, clothes horses, stools and simple pieces of furniture. With experience he progressed to charmingly crafted children's toys – carts, trucks, boats, whips and tops, kites, puzzles, and dolls houses, he also created other objects such as trinket boxes and decorative picture frames.

He had always refused to accept payment for his work; the pleasure in making the objects had been payment enough, but people found ways to show their gratitude. George and his wife had eaten countless home-made pies, cakes, biscuits, jams, chutneys and pickles donated by the delighted recipients.

George had given up his hobby several years ago when his hands became crippled with arthritis, nevertheless he was prepared to endure the pain in order to create a final and very special gift.

Methodically, he examined each piece of wood on his bench, expertly searching for knots and flaws. He had selected them with care and saved them for years, he knew they were perfectly suited for this particular project.

During the months that followed, the old man laboured

for several hours of each day. His progress was hampered by the increasing pain in his hands, which he did his best to ignore. There were days when he could barely hold his tools, but he forced himself to continue. Eventually the day arrived when he stood back and proudly admired his handiwork, it was by far the finest object he had ever made and finished just in time.

His son and grandson visited the following day on the occasion of his grandson's 5th birthday. George could hardly contain his excitement and after exchanging a few pleasantries with his son, he anxiously took his grandson by the hand and led him into the front room.

His grandson's eyes opened wide with amazement. 'Is that for me?'

The old man nodded.

With a cry of delight, the child clambered onto the back of the splendid rocking horse, he put his arms around the horse's neck and laid his cheek on its mane, his grandson clearly adored it.

George breathed a sigh of relief, it had been worth every moment of the pain; he could almost see the bond forming between them.

The boy thought for some time. 'Velvet! Her mane feels like velvet, so that's what I will call her.'

The weary old man nodded his agreement, it was a perfect choice.

Sadly George never knew of the immense pleasure Velvet

gave to his grandson, he died a few days later.

The old man carefully examined the dusty old rocking horse. The passage of time and several boisterous children had taken their toll.

The formerly glorious velvet mane was in tatters and the paintwork was cracked and peeling. The saddle and bridle were damaged beyond repair and would need replacing. The tail had been pulled off, two of the leg joints were badly damaged and the red bow base was spilt.

He had inherited his grandfather's love of wood and his skill for woodwork. Following several unrewarding jobs he had launched a business selling the wooden objects he had crafted. He hadn't made a fortune but had made enough money to marry, bring up five children and live comfortably from his profits and had built up a reputation locally as a quality craftsman.

He lost himself in thought as he remembered the day so long ago when his grandfather had given Velvet to him. He was well into adulthood before he understood that the old man had borrowed time in order to make the rocking horse for him. He silently stroked Velvet's shabby mane and deeply regretted his neglect, which had led her to this sorry state.

As he painstakingly restored Velvet to her former glory, his strong feelings of love for the rocking horse were re-awakened. As a child he was painfully shy and had few friends. It was natural that Velvet had become his confidante. He recalled the many one sided conversations with Velvet about his problems and fears, and his hopes and dreams. He talked to her as he worked, although his words were now concerned with getting old, pain and fear of death.

Exactly like George his grandfather, he was planning to give Velvet to his grandson for his 5th birthday. No one could understand better than he how thrilled his grandson would be with the gift.

A few days later he led his grandson into the spare room and presented Velvet to him.

'Wow!' thanks gramps.

'Her name is Velvet.'

'Cool.' his grandson clambered up and began rocking. 'This is great fun.' he said as he kicked his heels savagely into her flanks.

The old man turned and gazed vacantly out of the window.

'Her name is Velvet.' he repeated quietly.

At the end of the visit, when he saw Velvet being loaded onto the trailer the old man couldn't bear to watch. He busied himself with some small task until the sound of the engine starting made him look up.

As the vehicle moved forward the horse rocked backwards in response to the momentum and then slowly arched forward in a silent parody of a farewell gesture.

The old man who had endured more than his share of sorrow, hadn't given way to emotion since he was twelve, not even when his wife had died. He raised a hand in silent acknowledgement and felt a tear roll slowly down his cheek.

'Bye Velvet' he whispered.

Author's Note:

'Velvet' was brought to life thanks to a conversation with my elderly next-door neighbour - a lovely lady.

We talked at length on the subject of the good old days and the high value people held for their possessions compared to the attitude of today's 'throw away society'. I told her about my grandfather who looked after his possessions meticulously and kept them for years. He was a train driver and he made many toys for me when I was a child. I still use an ironing board to this day, which he made over 50 years ago.

George Black in this story was based on my grandfather's character.

Several months ago I read a very touching short tale about a rocking horse, which inspired the plot. I hope you enjoy it.

Lesley Truchet

Snow fell outside the kitchen window. It added feathery layers to the white blanket that covered the the picture postcard that was Lydgate brew. It was so quiet about it. I disregarded my coffee cup and finished cleaning my shot-gun. I watched Paul, my youngest son, rock back and forth from his stool while he haunched his tiny frame over the kitchen counter-top. He stuck his tongue out in determined artistry. Crayons and sheets of paper peppered the surface. He was having trouble recreating the sun. I sympathised. Yellow crayons were the worst. They never showed up on white paper very well. When I was a kid, I used to do an outline with a thin-tipped black marker to make the co-lour stand out. Colour doesn't need an outline in snow. Snow is a different kind of white. I loved to pee on it. The yellow was brilliant. There were other special effects, too; the faint hiss of snow-melt, acrid tendrils of steam rising alongside the expected zingy aroma, and the yellowed area sinking like a perverse footprint. Flick liked making snow angels. I liked pissing in the snow. We often argued the rel-ative merits of our personal tastes. Her family were from Tandle Hills. I don't think any of them had ever taken a piss outside. It takes all sorts to make a world, I guess.

The colour red is a whole different kettle of fish. Red crayons explode onto paper as waxy lumps of intensity to assault the eyeballs. If yellow is vibrant, red is something else, altogether. It's a colour I can hardly express. Red on snow is as bright and dark as space and as terrifying and thrilling as getting caught kissing; it's often too much to see to recall accurately. I remember Flick, though. The first time she saw red snow she puked. It hissed and steamed like piss, but it definitely wasn't yellow. The hot lumps in it sunk deeper in the snow than the wet bits did. In my memory I hear her crying. I don't think a person ever forgets the first time they made their wife cry. Of course, we were only ten at the time, and she was slumming it with her Aunt in Lees. Larry was there. We all met in Lees library and became an inseparable gang. We both had air rifles. We took her hunting crows, up Strinesdale. I shot one. It exploded. Flick cried and Larry laughed at her. I promised myself, there and then, I would look after her for the rest of my life, and I would not make her cry again.

"You need a marker to make the rays pop out," I advised Paul.

He looked up from the paper, as if he only just realised I was in the room. "Am I big enough yet?"

"For hunting?" I shook my head. "When your mother says it's okay, then it's okay."

"She says to quit asking."

"Then leave it a while."

"How long?"

"Ooh, I'd say until you're at least in double figures."

Paul's legs stopped swinging, the drawing instantly forgotten. The fire in his eyes mimicked the flare of his nostrils in outrage. "Ten?"

I swallowed a chortle, put the shotgun in its case and went over to look at his drawings. He let me ruffle his mop of unruly hair. "Hey, these are good! I like the one with the horse best."

"It's a cat."

"Of course it is. I still like it the best."

Chimes from the front doorbell announced Larry's arrival. I heard Flick's quick footsteps answer it with an urgency neither I nor the postman could usually elicit. I listened to the pair's muffled conversation. It dragged them along the hall at a funeral pace. I left the artist to his misery, grabbed my gun, hunting jacket and back-pack and met them in the hall. Guilty eyes scrambled over me for a moment before they found their footing.

"Hope you've got your thermals on." Larry grinned. He'd brought in a dose of cotton-fresh air that hit my nostrils like a slab of ice.

"Just be careful out there," Flick addressed us both. "I think you guys are crazy going out when the weather man says more snow's coming."

I put my arm around her waist and gave it a squeeze. "We won't take risks. I promise." She stiffened in my arms. It must have been uncomfortable for her to act dutifully in front of Larry. Another slice of pain assaulted my heart. I didn't know it had so much hurt left in it.

I felt her sad, desperate eyes bore into my back all the way down the driveway. I didn't look back. Larry fixed down a fluttering end of tarpaulin on the Land Rover without sneaking a peek at my wife. I wondered if she felt ignored. I slipped on a disregarded fast-food container as I swung into the passenger seat. Larry was meticulous in his ward-robe, housekeeping and working life, but a real slob when it came to his cars. He climbed in, ignored the chiming reminder to buckle-up and hit the ignition and radio at the same time. We left in a whirlwind of snow and rock music.

I looked back, but the snow was already erasing my life. Somewhere in the seamless join along the blank horizon our little house was swallowed up. I wondered how Flick would fill her time today.

We hit the back lanes, wriggling away from civilisation. The land around us was anonymous and repetitive. Songs devoured minutes and miles. Larry was concentrating on finding the road. There were no fresh tyre tracks to follow.

"Do you remember the first time we went hunting, Larry?"

My voice startled him, as if he'd forgotten I was there. He smiled. "The first time? How the hell should I remember that?"

"I remember. The snow was just like this. Flick, you and me went out with an air-gun, hunting crows."

"Yeah? Did we get any?"

I didn't answer. Larry swung the bonnet of the vehicle onto a private road. The snow hadn't quite won the right to fill it. The higher banks of land, either side, formed a protective barrier against snowdrifts. The Land Rover bowed and nodded to potholes full of black, muddied water as we drove along. We came to the clearing where the sanatorium used to be. It was just a shell. The roof had long gone, and the windows were naked of glazing. It was like this thirty years ago when the three of us hunted crows here. The only noticeable change over the decades was that the entire back wall had collapsed, leaving it looking like a theatre set instead of a building.

Larry turned off the engine, got out and peeled back the tarp. I got my kit together, too, and we strode through the ankle deep snow toward a wooded copse of trees where the hunting was good.

As was our practice, we took out our guns once we'd crossed a small stream. I loaded two shots and left the barrel broken to avoid accidents. Larry led the way, his gun ready, with only the safety to take off. We hunkered down and waited for what we hoped would not be long; there were fresh deer tracks.

I watched a bullish stream of breath puff out of Larry's nose in a steady rhythm. I wanted to punch him on it until the whirling clouds belched like a derailed steam-train. I wanted to split his skin with my bare knuckles, and watch his blood spatter the snow. I thought back to Paul's crayoning. He'd find it hard to see his mother cry. And she would cry if I hurt Larry. He was all she wanted now. It enraged me to think about how Larry had laughed at her squeamish reaction to the dead crow, all those years ago. How could she forget that, and how could she fall in love with someone who couldn't even remember her distress? Her horrified tears had changed me, made me see nothing but her, made me want nothing but to keep her safe, keep her smiling, hold her forever. Ever since the day I saw the two lovers together I wondered why she could smile into his eyes so trustingly. Had she considered his past record with women, or thought about the kind of life they would lead together? He would hurt her. He would shred her heart.

She would be left as torn as I was now. A thousand little

incisions would overwhelm her every time he dropped a careless word, cast a careless glance, or ignored a little plea from her soul. He'd kill her, crush her spirit, make her cry. Larry's breathing became faster. He nudged me. Up ahead a roebuck wove his way through the thicket on the other side of the clearing. He was majestic, in his prime. Larry stayed low and moved forward. He took the safety off his gun and waited for the animal's path to present the best shot. The roebuck was blind to us. As far as he was concerned all was well in his kingdom. He did not expect any threat. I closed the barrel on my own gun. For the briefest of moments Larry moved in front of my sights. I thought about pulling the trigger. I didn't. I felt sick. It was a fleeting thought, but it had existed. It shocked me. I think I gasped. I must have gasped. The roebuck bolted. Larry loosed a shot; the sharp crack disturbed a murder of crows in the tree line. They rose with caws of protest that aped the expletives punctuating the air around Larry until the retort from the gun receded.

Larry looked at me. He didn't look angry, just resigned in his frustration. I couldn't help but think his expression showed more than he meant it to. Every muscle in his face echoed his steady impatience. My presence was an immovable obstacle thwarting his every desire.

I couldn't stand the fact Flick cried when we were ten. I was not going to make her cry now. I would leave. Larry would not. They might be happy. I would tell her that night. I took the lead for the return to the Land Rover. Larry followed in silence.

The stream was in sight. I broke the barrel and stowed my gun. Larry did not. I heard him load two shots. I started to turn toward him.

"Please, don't turn around."

"You're going to shoot me, Larry?"

"Yes, and I am sorry about it, really I am, but I'm going to do it anyway."

I didn't have time to respond, or to fully turn my body toward him. He took the shot. He made it count, too. Bizarre, but it felt like getting kicked by an iron-shod donkey. I felt winded. I was rolling in the snow before the pain hit. Little balls of lead-shot peppered my side and shredded me with a thousand icy shards of pain. I couldn't get my breath to cry out. I kept on thinking about the time I broke a tooth on one. It was as I ate a roebuck's liver. It struck me how persistent those shot pellets were--the way they buried themselves everywhere. I thought of my liver, my heart, my lungs, and all the other living gloop that the good Lord shoved inside me. Would I die from blood loss or organ failure?

The sun was eclipsed by Larry's silhouette. I couldn't see his expression. I was glad of it. I hoped he was sorry. I hoped he was scared. I hoped he would fix this, fix me.

Larry left.

I heard the unmistakable belch of the Land Rover's engine compete with the radio station's latest rock classic, until both faded into the distance.

I hoped I would die with my eyes shut. The crows had come back, perhaps to dine on my gleaming, glassy delicacies. I seasoned them with some salty tears. It was not the only liquid leaking from me.

The air around me was leaden. I bench-pressed against it and managed to turn onto my side. The snow was corrupted and soiled. The filth of the wet woodland floor beneath its slush grubbied its way through Larry's retreating footprints. Tendrils of steam wafted like fairy-made vapour trails from the spreading port-stained puddle that emanated from my middle. The thickness of my blood fascinated me, as did its changing colour. It was deep crimson as it sat slightly proud of the snow's surface for a moment, before the melting snow diluted it to Slush-Puppie status. The ice changed the crimson to something akin to a pillar-box shade—vermilion, I think it's called. But, even then, it refused to give up the intensity. In fact, the more it melted the brighter the shade of red that dazzled from nature's canvass.

Paul's crayons could never do it justice.

I wanted to pee. Not because I felt the urge to pee, but because I reckoned that the yellow would be crazy intense against the red hue. When people eventually discovered my body, they'd be a little bit awestruck by the artistry, and not simply distressed by the horrifying spectacle. I didn't pee. I couldn't pee. A slow, creeping, numbness invaded my spine. I couldn't move anything, except the corners of my mouth, which turned up into a grin. Flick would not cry at my death, not even if she saw it up close in a police report or mirrored in the haunted musings of her lover's murderous gaze. No, she would not cry, because it was beautiful to behold: I was the ultimate snow angel. My life spilled out into fiery wings beside me. My pale skin aped a Renaissance painter's rendering of Gabriel in all his heavenly glory. I would see heaven. I had suffered my hell on earth. I had been a killer in my mind, but I had exercised my volition well. I sought redemption. I had forgiven the trespasses of others.

I wondered what the colours would look like.

Author's note

My father introduced me to guns. There was a regular clay-pigeon shoot up at the Roebuck pub at Strinesdale. I always assumed that this meant that there was no 'real' hunting, and men shot clays in preference to animals. I remember, with vivid horror, witnessing a real shoot in Derbyshire some years later—I never looked at a gun the same way again. Guns aren't for sport; they're for killing. Marriage can be much the same thing. I remember, with vivid horror, witnessing one partner's murder of another's love in a divorce some years later—I never looked at a promise the same way again. Love isn't for wimps; it's a front line assault of the battle-hardened romantic who knowingly faces death for the sake of a greater good.

Amanda Carr

THE WASHING LINE

"Will you just look at that."

"What am I looking at?"

"The washing line. Look at that."

"All I can see is that everything is shining white. What's wrong with that?"

"Look at how many pairs of knickers she's got. She must change hers every day."

"Er. Er. Well, so do I."

"But you're a teacher."

Author's note

This conversation actually took place; I found it memorable.

Marjory Travis

WATER

"Oh look at that water in the gutter. See how it's going faster as the slope gets steeper. How brown it is! They must be cleaning the pipes out. Oh there it goes, down the grid!"

"Do you want to go up and see the waterman? Hold my hand then. There must be something nasty in the water. They always do it here now because we're the first street off that branch from the waterworks. There he is. He has that big key to open the tap under ground. Ah look. The water is starting to run clearer. He'll be switching our water back on soon."

"Do you remember what happened when you were a little girl? Only a bit? I'm not surprised. You were very poorly. You'd been with aunty. She noticed you had gone very quiet and pale. Then you were hot and shaky, so she put you to bed and asked Granny Jones across the road to phone me and the doctor. She nipped down the back to the phone box."

"I came as quickly as I could. But by the time I got here you'd got sick and sleepy. As I walked up the street I heard Aunt Lucy saying to Granny Jones 'Bertha, I think she's passed on.' I couldn't believe my ears. It was the worst moment of my life."

"I snatched you out of her arms and cuddled you close. I kept thinking that if only I held you close enough, loved you enough, you would be all right. The doctor drove up at that moment. He was marvellous."

"Mind you for a day or two it was touch and go. We

moved your cot downstairs so that you'd be warmer and so someone could be near you all the time. And gradually you started to drink again and to eat a bit, but you didn't move much. The medicine the doctor gave you didn't taste very nice, but you took it very well like a good girl and it soon cleared the worms out."

"The doctor came again a few days later and I remember he walked into the kitchen and stood by the sink and told you to walk over to him – and you did. I nearly cried with joy. You were right again."

"We never found out everything, but it seems something had gone wrong at the waterworks and some untreated water had come through on our branch. Nobody was poorly but you. And they're a lot more careful these days."

"There now, he's finished. We'll have water again soon. You're thirsty now? You can't wait? Well never mind, the pop man came this morning. You can have some dandelion and burdock."

Author's note

One of my earliest memories is Dr Strang encouraging me to walk from my cot into the kitchen. The story was often related of the attack of worms and I was always struck by the emotion displayed by my notoriously unsentimental mother. Obviously I've changed a bit and added a bit to round out the story.

Maggie Nicholson